Patrick wasn't convinced he'd come to the right person

Nadine could see that, looking into his eyes.

Keeping her gaze direct and confident, she said, "Like I said earlier, finding missing persons is a specialty of our firm. As it happens, I'm between cases right now and I could start on this immediately."

Okay, technically that was a lie, but Nadine told herself it wouldn't matter, not as long as she found Patrick's son for him. Which she was determined to do.

Patrick's eyes held hers a moment longer, then he nodded. "Okay. Let's do it. What's the first step?"

She struggled to keep her excitement contained. "We sign a standard contract and you pay a retainer." She mentioned the base amount. When Patrick indicated his agreement, she asked him to wait while she drew up the papers.

"Too bad your receptionist isn't here to do that," Patrick commented.

Dear Reader,

When I started THE FOX & FISHER DETECTIVE AGENCY series, I knew that Nadine Kimble was destined to be more than a receptionist. She knew it, too. She's waited patiently for the opportunity to advance her career, only to be put off time and again.

What I love most about Nadine is that she turns her back on money and social status in order to follow her dream. And she steps well out of her comfort zone to make that dream happen.

Speaking of stepping outside her comfort zone, have I mentioned Patrick O'Neil? He's the kind of rugged hero you don't want to mess around with. So what's he going to say when he finds out the private investigator he hired to find his son is really the firm's receptionist?

I love hearing from readers, so send me an e-mail sometime. Also, do check my Web site, www.cjcarmichael.com, regularly for news about my next trilogy and to enter my "Surprise!" contests.

Happy reading!

C.J. Carmichael

Receptionist
Under Cover
C.J. Carmichael

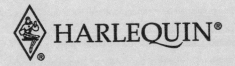

HARLEQUIN®

TORONTO • NEW YORK • LONDON
AMSTERDAM • PARIS • SYDNEY • HAMBURG
STOCKHOLM • ATHENS • TOKYO • MILAN • MADRID
PRAGUE • WARSAW • BUDAPEST • AUCKLAND

Recycling programs
for this product may
not exist in your area.

ISBN-13: 978-0-373-71623-4

RECEPTIONIST UNDER COVER

ABOUT THE AUTHOR

Hard to imagine a more glamorous life than being an accountant, isn't it? Still, C.J. Carmichael gave up the thrills of income tax forms and double-entry bookkeeping when she sold her first book in 1998. She has now written more than twenty-eight novels for Harlequin Books, and invites you to learn more about her books, see photos of her hiking exploits and enter her surprise contests at www.cjcarmichael.com.

Books by C.J. Carmichael

HARLEQUIN SUPERROMANCE

SIGNATURE SELECT SAGA

*Return to Summer Island
**Three Good Men
†The Fox & Fisher Detective Agency

With love to Mike Fitzpatrick…who never
turns his back on a good adventure

CHAPTER ONE

NADINE KIMBLE WATCHED as the office printer spewed out a certificate proving she'd aced the online private investigation course she'd been taking the past six months. She knew her boss—Lindsay Fox, founder of The Fox & Fisher Detective Agency—was in her office. It was now or never, unless she wanted to be a receptionist for the rest of her life. Which she didn't, since she was only twenty-seven and the rest of her life would hopefully involve many more decades.

With the certificate still warm in her hands, Nadine marched up to Lindsay's office, rapped briefly on the door, then opened it.

Lindsay wasn't alone. Her partner and fiancé, Nathan Fisher, was sitting in the chair usually reserved for clients, while she paced the room in bare feet, her high heels, as usual, strewn on the floor next to her desk. They were arguing in a civilized yet heated manner, and didn't stop on Nadine's account.

"Printed invitations are classier than e-mail, Fox. That's all I'm saying."

"I care about trees more than I care about 'class.' What do you think, Nadine? Should we send out stuffy printed invitations to our wedding—or speedier, cheaper and more environmentally friendly e-mail invitations?"

"We're having such a small wedding, all we need is a dozen invitations. What's that—a twig? Plus, we can use recycled paper."

"Nadine?" Lindsay asked.

"Oh, no. I'm not falling for this again." Nadine thought the printed invitations would be nice, but no way was she stating her opinion. Getting between Lindsay and Nathan in one of their "discussions" was never a good idea.

While Lindsay and Nathan loved each other passionately and made excellent business partners, they had opposite ideas about many subjects…especially their upcoming wedding.

And both of them sulked like kids if she took one side over the other.

"We've left this so late. The wedding is in two months." Lindsay flipped the pages on her day-timer. "Do we even have time to get something printed?"

"The only reason we're late is because you keep putting me off." Nathan leaned forward in his chair, planting both hands on his well-muscled thighs. "I have a friend with a graphic-design shop two blocks from here on Amsterdam. She said if we come over right now, she can help us choose a design and have the invitations in the mail in three days."

Lindsay made a face, then puffed out a sigh. "Fine. But the wedding cake will be chocolate. No fruitcake. No fancy white icing that tastes like plastic."

"What about carrot cake with thick cream-cheese icing?"

Lindsay's mouth tightened obstinately. "Chocolate."

Nathan looked as if he was going to argue some more. Then he changed his mind and nodded. "Printed invitations and chocolate wedding cake."

Lindsay reached for her shoes. "All right, then. I guess we better go talk to this friend of yours."

Nadine realized her opportunity was about to be lost—again. "Um, before you go, I wanted to discuss something."

"What's up?" Lindsay asked as she slipped into her heels. She was a practical woman with a weakness for impractical shoes. One of several quirks to her character that kept her interesting.

Nadine showed Lindsay her latest certificate. "I want to start working on my own cases. I think I'm ready."

The two partners exchanged a quick look, and Nadine, recognizing their skepticism, knew she had to speak fast. "I know you did me a favor, hiring me as a receptionist when I'd never held a job before."

She'd had only her liberal arts education, and a lot of experience planning dinner parties and charity galas for her wealthy parents. Her father had always planned for her to work for the Waverly Foundation after graduation, but at the last moment Nadine had rebelled.

She had a dream. Her parents thought it was silly, reckless and potentially dangerous.

But Nadine still wanted to be a private detective.

"Despite my lack of experience, I think I've done a good job."

"More like an excellent job," Lindsay said. "But there's a world of difference between working in an office and handling a case from start to finish."

"You already do a lot of our research and record keeping," Nathan added. "Plus you handle the calls from clients and keep track of us when we're out in the field. We really couldn't operate without you."

Nadine heard what they were saying, but she wouldn't be mollified. Not this time. "This is because I don't have police training, isn't it?"

Lindsay, Nathan and their third partner, Kate Cooper, had originally all worked at the Twentieth Precinct of the New York Police Department. "I've asked around. There are plenty of excellent P.I.'s in this city who didn't start out with the force."

"That's true." Lindsay ran her fingers through her delicately colored, blond hair. The blunt style ended at her jawline, emphasizing her determined chin. "I'm just not sure you're ready."

"But we're drowning in work," Nadine pointed out. "And Kate will be taking maternity leave soon." She and her commercial pilot husband, Jay Savage, were expecting their first baby in four weeks.

"We've been gradually increasing your investigative responsibilities," Nathan said.

"Yes. And I'm glad for everything you've thrown my way." She knew how to do background checks now, and she was often asked to do research for the others. "But I'm always in the office. Always behind my desk."

"But who would deal with the calls and the clients if you weren't there?" Lindsay asked.

Nadine swallowed. She wasn't quite brave enough to suggest that one of *them* could man the lines if she was out.

Nathan glanced at his watch. "We've got to get

going. Let's talk about this later when we have more time, okay?"

Same old story. Nadine sighed as they left. She had no illusions about what would happen later. More lip service to the notion of allowing her more responsibility. Then, in a couple of weeks, they would hire someone new, someone to cover for Kate, and Nadine'd be back to the same administrative jobs she always handled.

Nadine sank into her chair, frustrated. She loved working at Fox & Fisher. Lindsay, Nathan and Kate were friends, not just coworkers.

She didn't want to leave.

But at the same time, she had a dream, and she was ready. She might not be a rabble-rouser like Lindsay, or steely minded like Kate, but she had talents, too.

Nadine went to the coffee station to rinse out the pot and start a fresh brew. Making coffee, answering phones, checking stuff on the Internet and writing up reports—yeah, she was great at that stuff. She wanted more, though. And she knew she could do it.

But no one here was going to believe it because they all thought of her as a receptionist. Worse than that, their opinions were colored by her background—her rich family and privileged upbringing.

She knew they all wondered why she bothered to work at a "real" job. But Nadine had never been comfortable with her family's wealthy status. Far from giving her added confidence, the money had only made her less secure. She wanted to be valued as an individual, not as an heiress. That was why she used her mother's maiden surname at work, and why she rarely spoke about her Waverly family connections.

She was determined to prove—to others and to herself—that she could handle the job. But how could she do that if they never let her try?

Nadine studied the calendar on her computer, where she kept track of everyone's schedules. Knowing Nathan and Lindsay, it would take a while to find something they could agree on. Meanwhile, Kate had gone with Jay for her eight-month doctor checkup.

She would be alone in the office for a couple of hours.

Supposing, just supposing, a client should walk in the door during that time?

They didn't get drop-in business very often, but it did happen. Usually, if the others were out, Nadine would book an appointment and ask the potential client to come back later.

But what if, this time, she didn't?

Nadine put a hand to her chest. Her fingertips tingled with a rush of adrenaline, and her heart raced.

Dared she do it?

She had to. There was no other way. The next client who walked in the door was going to be hers.

PATRICK O'NEIL COULDN'T BE bothered with umbrellas. He just pulled his coat tighter against the cool November rain. Not to protect himself—he didn't mind the damp and he wasn't cold. Compared to Alaska, where he'd researched and written his last book, this weather was balmy. No, it wasn't his body he was trying to protect, but the letters.

He'd been watching the addresses of the brownstones as he walked along, and now he stopped. The sign was discreet, but it seemed he had arrived.

Feeling oddly self-conscious, he glanced left, then

right. No one even noticed him. Most of the passersby were huddled under umbrellas. And, anyway, New Yorkers always minded their own business.

He climbed six steps to a door that led to a small vestibule. The Fox & Fisher Detective Agency wasn't the only business housed in this building. He checked the signs, then climbed more stairs, up to the next story.

A semitranslucent door had *The Fox & Fisher Detective Agency* lettered over the glass. He checked the hours, confirmed that it was open. Well, of course it was. What business wouldn't be at three in the afternoon on a Tuesday?

He went in.

A woman was sitting at a reception desk. She was petite, with dark hair, darker eyes and pretty red lips. Her smile was meant to be welcoming, but she seemed slightly nervous about something.

"I don't have an appointment," he said. "Is that okay?" Up until three seconds ago, he hadn't been sure he would go through with this. He wasn't the kind of guy who hired other people to solve his problems.

Then again, he'd never had a problem quite like this one before.

"That's fine. I can fit you in without an appointment."

"Good. I'm in luck then." She had a beautiful, refined way of speaking. Well educated, he could tell.

He wasn't. He'd learned about life the old-fashioned way, through work and experience, and the lack of a college education had never stood in his way. He slipped his fingers inside his jacket, reached past the book he'd just received in the mail, to the manila envelope. Still dry. Good.

He removed his coat and folded it carefully over one arm, so the envelope wouldn't fall out.

"Would you like to hang that in the closet?"

He shook his head, the muscles in his arms tightening reflexively. "I'd rather keep it with me."

"Fine." The dark-haired woman picked up a stack of files, and for no reason that he could tell, moved them to a different corner of her desk. "How can I help you?"

He was standing there like a dolt, trying not to feel absurd, yet the situation was so surreal. He'd certainly never dreamed that he would have reason to seek out the services of a private investigator.

Yet here he was.

"I'm Patrick O'Neil. I'd like to speak with one of your investigators. I—I need to find someone."

"Locating missing persons is one of our specialties. And I'd be glad to help you. My name is Nadine Kimble."

"You? But—I assumed you were the receptionist."

Those pretty dark eyes blinked. "She's on a break. I was just filling in for a few moments. We can continue our discussion in the boardroom. Would you like a coffee?"

He nodded. This situation was just getting stranger and stranger. Coffee would help. He let her pour him a cup, then added his own cream before following her down a short hall to a room on the left.

Like the reception area, the conference room was decorated in a modern, minimalistic style. He squinted at the odd black-and-white photos on the wall.

"Close-ups of paper clips," the woman explained, which really explained nothing, as far as Patrick was concerned. Why put paper clips on your wall when you could have something truly beautiful, like a photograph of mountains, or the ocean or even one graceful tree?

"Please sit down and make yourself comfortable." Nadine Kimble opened a notebook and pulled out a pen. "Now—who would you like us to find?"

He had an urge to question her credentials, but he supposed that was sexist of him. Just because she was little and cute and extremely feminine didn't mean she couldn't be a kick-ass investigator. Plus, this was the place that had been recommended.

With care, he removed the items in his coat pocket, first the book, then the package. Her eyes fell on the book. It was upside-down and his author photo was clearly visible.

"Is that you?" She reached across the table. "May I look?"

Action and Adventure in New Zealand was his sixth book. This ought to be old hat to him by now. But he still felt a rush of pride at seeing his picture, and his name, right there on the cover.

"By all means. I just received that copy from my publisher. The book won't be available in stores for another month."

"So, you're an author. Of travel books."

She sounded impressed.

Many women were.

This is not some girl you're trying to chat up at the bar. Still, he found himself giving her his regular spiel. "I prefer to think of it as adventure travel. For people who are fit and up for a challenge and want to explore new places in ways that most tourists never experience."

"That sounds wonderful." She flipped through the

pages, stopping to look at some of the pictures. Then she gave him a rueful smile. "I'm sorry. I'm getting distracted, aren't I?"

She set the book to the side, then folded her arms on the table and leaned in toward him. "Tell me why you're here." She glanced expectantly at the manila envelope he'd placed on the table.

He covered the envelope with a protective hand. He felt as if something thick and hard had suddenly lodged in his throat. Even though he'd already decided this was the most expeditious solution, he suddenly wasn't sure he could share his very personal situation with a stranger.

But what choice did he have? The revisions on his Alaska manuscript were due at the publishers in three weeks. He had no time to handle this himself. Wasn't even sure how to go about it, truth be told.

"I need your help to—" His voice cracked. He took a sip of coffee, then managed to get the rest out. "To find my son."

CHAPTER TWO

NADINE STARED AT THE MANILA envelope on the table, her feet suddenly as cold as ice.

Was this case going to be something she could handle on her own? What would she do if it wasn't?

She'd been hoping her first client would be a nice, old lady, missing a piece of antique jewelry. Or maybe a sweet, young husband, worried that his new wife was unfaithful. Of course, in Nadine's imagination, she wasn't....

But instead she'd ended up with this strong, forceful man brimming with masculine vitality. Patrick O'Neil seemed not quite wild, but close to it, with thick, unruly, chestnut-colored hair, and a body packed with solid muscles.

She'd never met anyone like him, and felt completely out of her element. For heaven's sake, he was an adventurer by trade. The book he'd just shown her had a picture of a guy paragliding off a cliff and she had no doubt that it was Patrick O'Neil himself in the photograph.

She swallowed, desperate to moisten her parched mouth. She couldn't let him see that she was intimidated. After all, he was here because he needed help.

"Your son...has he run away?" she asked, trying to

sound as if she'd seen it all and didn't expect to be surprised.

He seemed impatient as he shook his head. "Not really. The situation is complicated. Six weeks ago, when I left on a working trip to Alaska, I didn't even know I had a son. I found this envelope piled up with the rest of the mail that had collected over the six weeks I was away."

From the larger envelope, he pulled out two smaller letters. One of them had been opened. The other—addressed simply to Stephen—still sealed.

Puzzled, Nadine waited for him to explain.

"These letters were written by an old girlfriend. One was addressed to me, the other to a young man named Stephen." He ran a hand through his already mussed hair. "A young man she claims is my son."

Again Nadine struggled to keep her expression neutral, as if she ran across situations like this all the time. "And is he?"

He shrugged. "I assume so. June Stone and I dated in our senior year of high school. After graduation, she went to university, while I worked until I had enough money for my first trip to Europe. We'd always known we had different plans, so our breakup was inevitable."

"Where does the baby fit in?"

"Apparently June was pregnant when we broke up."

"And you didn't know?"

"No. In her letter, June said she decided not to tell me because she didn't want me to feel like she was trying to trap me into marriage."

"I assume she kept the baby?"

"Yes. She named our son Stephen and raised him on

her own. He's eighteen years old now, and he doesn't even know I exist."

"June must have told him something about his father."

"Apparently she led him to believe that his father was dead." Patrick shifted anxiously in his seat. "She said when he was young, she didn't have the courage to tell him the truth, and once she became ill, she didn't have the strength."

"I see." Perhaps June had been telling him the truth. But Nadine knew it was her job to be skeptical, to accept nothing at face value. "So why contact you now?"

"In a way, she didn't. This letter was mailed post-humously."

Nadine felt her eyes widen and quickly glanced down so he wouldn't see her surprise. "I'm sorry."

He nodded, accepting her brief statement of condolence. "Apparently it was her wish that these letters were to be mailed to me after her death. As soon as I read the one addressed to me, I went on the Web and found her obituary. She died of cancer five weeks ago."

His story was sounding like something from a movie, poignant and romantic. Nadine reminded herself that her job was to be objective and analytical. "Why do you think she wanted you to know about Stephen now?"

"She felt that since her son no longer had a mother, he might need a father." He shook his head. "She asked if I would contact Stephen and deliver this second letter in person."

Nadine eyed the unopened envelope. Why hadn't June asked for that letter to be mailed directly to Stephen? There was only one reason she could think of.

"She didn't want her son to know the truth unless you were prepared to meet with him."

"Exactly. Whether Stephen and I strike up a relationship is up to us, June wrote, but she did say she'd be grateful if I would help Stephen financially, with his university education, since her long illness depleted her financial resources."

"Ah." At the mention of money, Nadine's back straightened. Had June Stone been aware of Patrick's successful writing career? Possibly she'd stretched the truth a little—or a lot—in an effort to provide some financial security for her son.

Still, Patrick didn't seem to doubt the truth of her story. Not one word of it.

"You said the letter was mailed posthumously. By whom?"

"I have no idea. The return address is the apartment in Chelsea where June and her son used to live. The place has since been let to someone else."

He shook his head. "I wish that I'd kept in touch with June. For a while after we separated we kept up a correspondence. I sent her postcards from my travels and every Christmas she mailed a card to me care of my mother's address. But after a few years, that stopped. I hadn't heard from her in years. Until this."

"So now you want to talk to Stephen Stone?"

"Yes. Only I have no idea where to find him. The letter didn't provide any contact information." He unfolded two sheets of paper that looked as if they had been read over many times.

"May I read that?"

He hesitated, then passed it over. "I'm not even

sure her son lives in Manhattan. As I mentioned, he left
the apartment he lived in with his mother. I also phoned
the funeral home listed in the obituary, but they
couldn't help me."

Nadine glanced up from June Stone's handwritten
lines. "I assume you checked the phone listings?"

He nodded. "I called every S. Stone I could find.
And I searched the Internet, including Facebook. I can't
find him anywhere."

"That's unusual, for someone his age, though he
could be using a nickname on Facebook. Some kids
do."

"Yeah. That's what I figured. I'm kind of at a dead end
here and I don't have much time, since I'm on a tight
deadline with my next book. Do you think you can help?"

He looked her straight in the eyes, and Nadine could
see that he wasn't totally convinced that he'd come to
the right person.

Keeping her gaze direct and confident, she nodded.
"Like I said earlier, finding missing persons is a specialty of our firm. As it happens, I'm between cases right
now and I could start on this immediately."

Okay, technically that was a lie, but Nadine told herself it wouldn't matter, not as long as she found Patrick's
son for him. Which she was determined to do.

Patrick's eyes held hers a moment longer, and then
he nodded. "Okay. Let's do it. What's the first step?"

She struggled to keep her excitement contained. "We
sign a standard contract and you pay a retainer." She mentioned the base amount, figuring this case probably
wouldn't take very long. When Patrick indicated his agreement, she asked him to wait while she drew up the papers.

"Too bad your receptionist isn't here to do that," Patrick commented.

She was halfway to the door when he said that. She paused briefly and glanced back at him.

From his expression it seemed there had been no double meaning to his words, so she smiled and nodded. "That's okay. It won't take me long."

Fifteen minutes later, the business between them was concluded. "I'll call you in a couple of days and let you know how things are progressing," she promised as she passed him his copy of their agreement.

His chest expanded on a full breath. "Okay. So…any idea how long it will take to find Stephen?"

"That depends on several factors. But normally, in a case like this, we have results in three or four days."

She could see the relief on his face and knew she'd finally won him over.

"Great," he said. "I'll look forward to hearing from you then."

One last time their gazes connected, and she felt again the power of his presence. She sensed he had a mental toughness to match the physical perfection of his athletic body. But this letter from his old girlfriend had exposed a hint of vulnerability in him, too. And oddly it was that element about him that she found most appealing.

Following the example she'd seen set many times by the other partners at Fox & Fisher, Nadine escorted Patrick to the door. With a final confident handshake, she saw him on his way, and only once the door was firmly closed and she was alone again, did she allow herself to believe what had finally happened.

She'd done it! She'd signed her first client.

HALF AN HOUR LATER, KATE called to say that her doctor's appointment was over. "I'm going to stop by the office for some files, then call it a day. Did anything interesting come up this afternoon?"

"Not really." Nadine's conscience squirmed at the fib. As soon as she got off the line, she rearranged her files, so that her nameplate was visible again. That had been her only mistake, she thought, that she hadn't noticed quickly enough that the sign was in view. Fortunately, Patrick didn't seem to have noticed.

Then she went to the conference room to clear away the used coffee mugs. That was when she noticed that he'd forgotten his book. She took it with her to her desk, where she sat and studied the author photo on the back.

No question about it. The man was incredibly masculine, with a body that was all muscle, skin that was tanned and windblown, and eyes that were as blue as the New Zealand sky on the cover of his book.

She'd have to return this copy to him at their next meeting. In the meantime, she'd get busy finding his son...or the boy June Stone *claimed* was his son.

Take nothing at face value, Nathan and Lindsay had taught her. Check every fact, at least once, better yet twice. Never cut corners.

With their advice in mind, Nadine started to work, laying out a plan of action that would hopefully lead her to Stephen Stone.

Fifteen minutes later, she was interrupted as Kate walked in. The eight-months-pregnant detective was wearing a cleverly styled trench coat she'd bought from a discount maternity shop, but nothing could hide the huge ball of baby on her tall, normally thin frame.

"Oh, God, I'm tired." She pulled off the coat and hung it on her usual hanger. Her luxurious red hair was pulled in a messy knot at the back of her head and if she'd applied any makeup that morning, it was now worn off.

Still, she had a beautiful glow, Nadine thought. And she knew Jay felt the same way about his wife. Every time she'd seen them together, he'd been doting on her. "How was the appointment?"

"Everything's good. Though my doctor says the baby's head has already dropped into the birth canal, which is early given that the little peach isn't due for another month."

Kate frowned as she glanced at Nadine's computer screen. "What's that?"

"Just some research I'm doing for Nathan." The fibbing seemed to come easier each time she had to do it. "He and Lindsay have agreed to give me more case work. So if you ever have something you'd like a hand with—"

"Sure, Nadine. Thanks for the offer." Kate snagged a bottled juice smoothie from the fridge then headed back to her office, across from the conference room.

Despite her easy agreement, Nadine doubted if Kate was going to throw any work her way. If she did, it would only be basic research work, the kind that could be done from the safety of her desk at the office.

She was dying to get out in the field, performing surveillance, shooting video of suspects, interviewing witnesses…

She wondered if she'd get to do any of that with

Patrick O'Neil's case. She wanted to find his son quickly, but hopefully not *too* easily. Nathan always said to start a case by listing what you *did* know, then make a list of what you needed to find out.

She was still working on the first list when Lindsay and Nathan returned from their wedding planning.

"Did you select invitations?" she asked cautiously. The two of them seemed fairly relaxed and cheerful, so hopefully the appointment had gone well.

"They'll be in the mail by Monday," Nathan announced happily. "You should get yours next week."

"While we were out, we also ordered the cake." Lindsay hung up her jacket, then went for some coffee. "We're having two—white chocolate mousse cake, and devil's delight double cocoa cake."

"Those sound amazing."

Nathan, who was practically a vegetarian and generally avoided foods laden with fat or sugar, shivered. "Not to me they don't, but I'm glad you girls are happy." He kissed Lindsay, and they shared a mushy smile.

Then Lindsay asked if there had been any messages.

Nadine handed one slip of paper to Nathan and two to Lindsay.

"Anyone else call?" Nathan asked.

She swallowed. Here it was—another lie. "No. Just those three."

"Great." Lindsay had already ducked back into her office and Nathan was heading for his, when he noticed Patrick O'Neil's book on her desk. "Hey, I heard O'Neil had something coming out on New Zealand. Where did you find this?"

Oh, crap. "It was a gift," she improvised.

"Mind if I take a quick look through? Lindsay and I are considering New Zealand for our honeymoon."

Nadine couldn't think of any way to refuse that wouldn't sound suspicious. "Go ahead," she said, while at the same time berating herself for not hiding the darned book in a drawer. If she was going to keep Patrick's case secret until it was solved, she was going to have to start being a lot more circumspect.

AT SIX O'CLOCK, NADINE reluctantly turned off her computer and tucked her notes on the O'Neil case into her bottom drawer, under the pair of flat-soled shoes she kept on hand for emergencies.

Patrick's contract and his check were there, too. She wouldn't give the check to Nathan—who had taken over the accounting as soon as he became a full partner—until after she'd solved the case and come clean about what she'd done.

What a lot of fun it was going to be to see the expressions on everyone's faces when they realized she really could handle an entire case all on her own.

Nadine was pumped and didn't want to stop working, even though it was after five. But she'd promised her mother she would attend one of her charity galas that evening. The cause *de jour* was saving the rain forest, Nadine thought, with a heavy sigh. It wasn't that she didn't care about the rain forest, or the many other worthwhile causes her mother championed.

It was only that, in her opinion, the galas should be scrapped and the thousands of dollars it took to throw those big, fancy parties should be donated to the cause.

Her mother said her views were "shortsighted."

And maybe she was right. Maybe in ten or twenty years, Nadine would be signing up to join the boards of all these committees and worrying about decorating themes and menus and ticket sales.

But she hoped not.

She and her mother thought differently about so many topics that long ago she'd realized she could either speak her own mind and be estranged from her mother, or keep her opinions to herself.

Because she loved her mother, for the most part Nadine kept her opinions to herself. And attended the parties. And wore the dresses. And dated the men. It was just easier that way.

Two hours later, Nadine was in a strapless black gown in the ballroom of the Waverly Hotel on Park Avenue. The man whose arm she was holding was an up-and-coming lawyer who had done some work for her father.

His name was Trenton Oberg, and he already had three strikes against him.

He wasn't muscular.

His eyes were brown.

And his hair wasn't windblown in the slightest.

On the positive side of the equation, the food promised to be good and her cousin Liz was in attendance, so there was sure to be some shocking event or another to entertain the masses. Liz did not enjoy being in the background, ever.

Trenton let go of her arm to snag two glasses of champagne from a passing waiter. He handed her one, then clinked his flute against hers. "To a wonderful evening, with a wonderful girl."

The words were spoken glibly, without a trace of

sincerity, and Nadine smiled politely before taking a sip. Then a longer drink. Sometimes champagne was the only thing—

She sputtered as she caught sight of a man with a headful of dark brown hair that glittered with red highlights. He had his back to her, but the color of his hair, not to mention the cut of his suit—those wide shoulders and that impossibly slender waist—made her flashback to the man she'd met in the office today.

But why would Patrick O'Neil be at a high-society charity gala? She pulled on Trenton's sleeve.

He frowned slightly, then leaned in toward her. "What's wrong?"

"Do you know who's speaking tonight?"

He named a local dignitary who had been a friend of her family's for as long as she could remember.

"Anyone else?"

"Well, there's that action-adventure travel writer, Patrick O'Neil. But you wouldn't have heard of him."

Patrick O'Neil. Oh, Lord. Nadine could feel the skin at the back of her neck tingle. She had to get out of here before he noticed her.

But no sooner did she have that thought than Patrick turned around—and with an uncanny instinct, as if he'd sensed her thinking about him—looked her square in the eyes.

CHAPTER THREE

PATRICK HAD EXPECTED TO BE bored, and he'd been prepared for it. What he hadn't remembered was how damn uncomfortable formal attire could be. His feet—used to cushioned, merino wool socks and thick rubber soles—ached in these thin leather shoes. And the buttons on his tuxedo shirt seemed to tighten their hold on his neck with every minute.

He scanned the room in search of something that might distract him from his misery. Drinking wouldn't be smart. Not when he had to speak in about an hour.

Definitely lots of beautiful women here. But he felt little interest in trying to meet one of them. That letter from June…it had really knocked him for a loop.

Wait a minute. Over in the corner. He couldn't help staring at the pretty brunette with sparkling dark eyes. She was slender and utterly feminine…like a modern-day princess in a strapless dress that showed off flawless skin and an intriguing hint of cleavage.

She had a delicate beauty that set her apart from the many other gorgeous women in this room. But that wasn't the only reason she'd caught his attention. He had the feeling he'd met her before.

And then it hit him. Hell. She was the investigator from Fox & Fisher. Nadine Kimble.

At the very moment he recognized her, she glanced through the crowd, making contact with his eyes. Or maybe he imagined it, because now, a second later, she was looking just slightly to his left. Lowering her eyes, she took a very long drink from her champagne flute.

She'd looked completely different earlier today in a conservative skirt and high-necked sweater. Her hair had been straight and controlled and her makeup subdued.

But he was now quite certain she was the same woman.

He was already moving through the crowd, curious to find out why a detective from Fox & Fisher was mingling with New York City's wealthiest and most influential citizens. The tickets for tonight's event were a thousand bucks a head. Not something that fit into the average woman's budget, that was for sure.

Perhaps she had a rich boyfriend.

And at just that moment Patrick spotted him—a tall, academic-looking man in his late twenties, with dull eyes and an expression devoid of good humor. As Patrick watched, Nadine stood on her toes to speak into his ear. He nodded, then took her champagne flute and headed off, presumably for a refill.

She was alone now. And though she was no longer looking in his direction, he sensed she was aware of his approach.

Patrick wondered why he felt it was so important to speak to her. Not enough time had passed for her to have turned up any information about his son. Yet, he pressed on, weaving through the knots of people, drawing nearer, finally close enough to touch her lightly on the shoulder.

"MR. O'NEIL." NADINE SHIVERED, though the man's touch on her skin was warm. She swiveled ninety degrees, so she was almost, but not quite, facing him. "This is a surprise. I didn't realize you were tonight's speaker until just recently."

She clasped her hands behind her back to hide her trembling. She had to get rid of him. Fast. It wouldn't take Trenton long to refill their glasses, and when he returned she'd be obligated to make introductions, and her cover would be blown.

She could just imagine what her client would say when he found out her father was one of the owners of this hotel, her mother on the fundraising committee for this event.

"Call me Patrick. Please. Believe me, this isn't my usual habitat." He gave a desultory tug to his bow tie. "But my publicist went to a lot of work to arrange this gig and threatened to feed me to lions if I didn't show up."

"I guess it's good timing. With your new book coming out soon and all." She glanced over his shoulder, relieved to see that Trenton wasn't yet in the vicinity.

"Exactly. Still, it's ironic, isn't it? A big, fancy bash like this—everyone in expensive duds, eating exotic food. If we really cared about the rain forest, we'd be consuming less, not more."

That was exactly how she felt about the situation. But she couldn't afford to exchange political and social views with this man. She had to leave. Now.

"I must admit, I was surprised to see you here," Patrick continued.

She knew he was waiting for an explanation. Suddenly one came to her. She stepped closer to him and in a low voice said, "I'm attending on business. I'm sorry I can't explain further."

"Oh." Patrick's eyes widened. "You're undercover, then?"

She nodded.

"Well, I wouldn't want to mess things up."

"Exactly. Thanks so much for understanding." She squeezed his arm, in a gesture of farewell, and though she knew he was in excellent physical condition, she was still surprised to feel the tight resistance of muscle under the soft wool of his tux.

"We'll talk soon," she promised, before slipping off into the crowd. Not five steps later, a friend of her mother's called out her name, but she pretended not to hear as she hurried to put distance between herself and Patrick.

She'd slipped out of that predicament, but only barely. She didn't dare stick around for the entire evening. She was too well known here, had too many connections.

She would find Trenton and make an excuse to leave. There would be hell to pay from her mother, but there was no way around it.

THE NEXT MORNING NADINE WENT to the office early, despite not having slept well the night before. Granny Kimble had always said a clean conscience was essential to a good night's sleep, and now Nadine knew that was true. She'd never in her life told as many lies as she had in the past twenty hours.

Seeing Patrick last night had been an unexpected complication, requiring yet more little white lies on her part. She could so easily have been busted. Luckily she'd managed to exit fairly quickly after being spotted.

But part of her wished she could have stayed. She would have liked to hear him speak. Then maybe later, after the dinner, he would have sought her out for a dance. She imagined the band playing something slow and romantic, Patrick's arms tightening around her back…

Oh, Lord. What was she doing? Daydreaming about her client was definitely not professional.

She was up to her neck in deception, and the only way out was to solve this case, which meant finding Patrick's son, the sooner the better.

That was why she'd arrived so early. Hopefully she'd have the office to herself for at least an hour before the others arrived. Prior to her pregnancy, Kate had been an early bird, but these days she usually started her days at nine, like Lindsay and Nathan.

Yesterday Nadine had mapped out a strategy and now she reviewed her notes. The first step was checking out Stephen's mother—Patrick's old girlfriend—June Stone.

She located June's obituary on the Internet and read it carefully. June's parents had predeceased her, but she had been survived by a sister and her family, who lived in Boston, as well as her son, Stephen.

Nadine copied out the sister's name, then read on. The write-up on June's life was short, highlighting her career as a professor at Columbia University, and citing her business and masters degrees from NYU. The obit ended on a personal note… "In her spare time June loved skiing with her son and hiking with friends in the Berkshires."

And that was all the obituary had to offer.

Next, Nadine tracked down June's last-known address, the apartment in Chelsea. What had happened with her furniture and belongings? Nadine wondered. Did her son have them?

Nadine tucked her hair out of the way as she tried to think what she should do next. Since Stephen didn't have a listed phone number or address that she could find, it might be smart to try and reach the sister, who would be his aunt.

She was about to start searching for a Boston phone listing, when the door opened and Kate stepped in, her freckled face pink from the cold, or exertion or possibly both.

She paused and sighed, hand on belly. "God, I wish we were on the ground floor."

Nadine had a sudden urge to tell Kate what she was doing. The others often brainstormed with one another about their cases. But unfortunately, she couldn't allow herself that luxury.

"Only four more weeks," she said encouragingly. "Then you'll be on mat leave with your beautiful baby."

"I can't wait." Besides being smart, coolheaded and ambitious, Kate also had a huge maternal streak and Nadine doubted if this would be her and Jay's only child.

She was mildly envious of the other woman's happiness. In her mind Kate had it all: a terrific husband, a great career and soon a baby, as well. Nadine wanted all those things, too, but she wanted to earn them, not have them handed to her on a silver platter by her parents.

Her mother didn't understand. She thought Nadine should be happy to work as an administrator for the family's charitable foundation and date the suitable young men introduced to her by her parents.

Both her mother and her father were still cool to the

fact that she was working at Fox & Fisher, but Nadine hoped that eventually they would accept that this was her chosen path. Maybe, at some point, they would actually be proud of her.

As soon as Kate was in her office, Nadine returned to her Internet search. She had to follow a winding trail to locate a phone number for June's sister in Boston, but eventually she was successful. No sooner had she punched the numbers into her cell phone than Nathan appeared.

Quickly Nadine shut her phone, then slid her papers under a stack of files.

"Hey, Nathan. Where's Lindsay?" They usually came to work together.

"I talked her into sleeping late. She had a bad night."

He didn't need to say more. Nadine nodded sympathetically. While Lindsay was strong, brave and capable, she and her sister, Meg, had been orphaned very young. The scars from their parents' violent deaths had left a mark on each of the girls.

For Lindsay, her personal demons included nightmares and insomnia—though from what Nadine had heard, both were becoming less frequent. But moments of high emotion could bring on a relapse.

"Is it the wedding?" Nadine speculated.

"I think so. I wonder if we should have just eloped like she said she wanted."

"It's still an option."

"Yeah. But I don't want her to feel cheated ten years from now. You know—that she didn't have the full deal on her wedding day."

Nadine smiled. Nathan couldn't help being himself. Any job worth doing, was worth doing well, in his opinion. And obviously that included weddings. "I'm sure your wedding will be perfect."

"As long as we end up as husband and wife, that will be perfect enough for me. From now on, I swear, I'm going to agree with everything Lindsay wants."

He hung up his coat, then went to pour himself a coffee. "I'm sorry we had to rush our conversation yesterday. Lindsay and I were talking last night. You're very important to this office. You know that, right?"

"That's good to hear. But—"

"You're ready for more. Right. We get that. And you will get more. But gradually. When Kate has her baby, we'll talk again. Maybe there will be a few cases of hers that you can take over."

There were still too many *maybes* in his proposition for Nadine's taste. But she smiled and thanked him anyway. Soon Nathan, Lindsay and Kate were going to realize that she was a lot more capable than they thought.

TWO DAYS LATER, NADINE HAD a problem. Finally she had some concrete results to share with Patrick, and she needed to arrange a meeting. But it couldn't be at the office. She couldn't count on one of the partners not walking in on her.

She pondered her options for a while, then sent him a text message, suggesting they go for coffee in Chelsea at the end of the workday. If she closed up the office at five and took a cab rather than the subway, she ought to be able to make it by six.

She'd just hit the send button, when Lindsay came out of her office. "Want to cut out early today? Nathan's planning on working late, so he can lock up the place.

Meg and I are going to shop for my wedding dress and shoes. When we're done, we'll go out for dinner."

Oh, heck. That sounded like fun. Nadine checked her silent phone and wondered if Patrick would respond soon. "I'd love to, but…"

Lindsay had noticed her glance at her phone. "Family plans?"

Nadine swallowed. She hadn't counted on needing to lie quite this often. She really didn't like it. Fortunately her phone chimed at just that moment and she held up a hand for Lindsay to wait.

She scanned the short message from Patrick: *Six is good for me.*

Patrick's speedy reply gave her a rush of excitement. She was looking forward to seeing him, and it wasn't just about the case. A lot of guys looked great in a tux, but he had looked really, *really* great. Not that it mattered. Only…she couldn't stop thinking about him.

She pressed a hand to her chest. She had to stop this. She was almost positive that professional investigators did not think about their clients this way.

She realized Lindsay had been watching her. Now, the astute investigator smiled wickedly. "No, it's not family. It's a hot date, isn't it? Go ahead and say yes, Nadine. We can go for dinner anytime."

"But, your gown and shoes…" Picking out a spectacular wedding outfit was the one thing that Lindsay seemed to be excited about and Nadine was honored to be invited along.

"Don't worry. I already know which dress I want. I'm just showing Meg so she'll think I've asked for her opinion."

"What about Kate?"

"Poor thing is too tired. She has a meeting in half an hour and then she's going straight home to put her feet up." Lindsay sighed. "Face it, we could have timed this wedding better. As it stands, Kate's baby is going to be only a few weeks old when we tie the knot."

"You didn't know Kate was pregnant when you set the date," Nadine reminded her. "And at least the office is slow between Christmas and New Year's, so your timing is good from that perspective."

"True enough."

Guilt tugged at Nadine again. Earlier Lindsay had mentioned she'd like help finding the right shoes. "Are you sure you won't need me tonight?"

"Definitely. Go out and have fun. I'll see you tomorrow."

As soon as Lindsay had left on her shopping trip, Nadine replied to Patrick's text: *Six is good. Meet at A Subway entrance at 14th Street.*

Less than a minute later, she received his reply: *Got it. See you there.*

Nadine swallowed. This was it. No backing out now.

CHAPTER FOUR

NADINE LEFT THE OFFICE promptly at five o'clock, anxious to be on time for her clandestine meeting with Patrick O'Neil. As she hurried down the stairs, briefcase in hand, she felt sophisticated and mysterious. After over a year of working at Fox & Fisher, she was finally an "operative" with her own "case." She felt like the main character in one of the detective stories she loved so much, and she was even dressed for the part with her classic trench coat and oversize sunglasses.

She'd chosen to meet in Chelsea for several reasons. First, the subway stop was only two blocks from the apartment where June Stone had lived with her son. She thought Patrick might be interested in walking by the place, and if he wasn't, she would do it alone once their meeting was over.

More important, she was reasonably certain that she wouldn't run into anyone she knew in Chelsea. None of the partners at Fox & Fisher lived or were working in the area. Nor was she likely to encounter one of her family members, or friends of her parents, any of whom would give her away in an instant.

When she dashed into a cab, it was raining lightly. By the time she emerged at the meeting spot, the rain had turned into miserable November snow. Nadine stamped her feet to keep warm and hoped Patrick wouldn't be late. She was wearing a wool dress and leggings under her coat, a hat and leather gloves, yet the damp chill seemed to seep through all of it.

At precisely six o'clock he showed up. She spotted him from a block away. He was wearing a dark coat with the top buttons undone, no scarf or hat, yet he didn't look the least bit cold. Watching him approach, she was struck again by his rugged good looks and the athletic grace of his body. Probably thanks to lots of sun and wind, he looked all of his thirty-six years. His age had been on his bio in the book.

But there was no gray in his hair and certainly he had more energy than anyone she'd ever met.

He shook her hand when he reached her. His blue eyes fixed on her steadily. "It's nice to see you again. I wasn't expecting results so quickly."

He was a little nervous, she realized. Good. Maybe he wouldn't notice that she was, too. "We're only a few blocks from June Stone's old apartment. I wondered if you'd like to take a look before we have our coffee."

"Yes. I didn't think it was coincidence that you'd suggested we meet here."

They set out heading west and Patrick was the first to speak. "I looked for you the other night. Later, after the speeches."

"I'm sorry. I would have enjoyed hearing your talk, I'm sure. But I had to leave before dinner was served."

He glanced at her, clearly intrigued. "I don't suppose you can give me any details about the case?"

"I'm afraid not. We're very strict about confidentiality at Fox & Fisher."

"Which is a good thing." He touched her elbow as they crossed the street. She found the gentlemanly gesture rather sweet, and unexpected, from a man she suspected cared little for most social graces.

But then, he'd seemed very comfortable in his tux the other night.

"Do you attend a lot of charity balls?" she asked.

"I try not to. In fact, after the other night, I called my publicist and said that was the last one. The people who go to these things mean well, I'm sure. But they're so caught up in the cycle of consume, consume, consume. They listen to my talk and don't even recognize that their lifestyle is part of the problem."

Having struggled with the same issues for most of her life, Nadine had to agree with him. Her mother put pressure on her to attend these functions, but each one seemed to require more effort than the last.

"Well, this is it." She stopped in front of a three-story apartment building. Counting out the units, she pointed to the window near the corner. "I think that was where June and Stephen lived."

Patrick stuffed his hands into his pockets and stared at the window for a long time. The curtains were drawn, but the interior lights were on and every now and then a shadow flickered as someone walked by.

"My son grew up here," he said, his voice hoarse. He glanced around the block, taking in the convenience store across the street and a coffee shop on the corner. Both were probably places June Stone—and Stephen—had spent a lot of time in.

"Want to try that place?" he asked, pointing at the coffee shop. It was on the corner of Ninth Street. Rafaella's was printed in white letters on a black awning over the window.

"Sure." She started in that direction, then stopped. Patrick was still gazing at the third-floor window.

"I suppose June thought she was doing me a favor by raising our son alone. But she should have told me."

JUNE'S DEATH WAS HAVING a profound effect on Patrick. She wasn't the first of his contemporaries to pass away. That would have been Jed, who'd died in an avalanche, a day after Patrick had skied the same terrain. Jed's passing had been hard, but finding out about June was even harder.

She had been his first love. And now, he was just discovering, the mother of his child.

June had been a straightforward person, intelligent and practical. At eighteen, she'd been cute, but it wasn't really her looks that had drawn him so much as her outgoing personality and her love of sports. She'd played volleyball and basketball and he'd liked the fact that she could shoot a basket just as well as he could.

He'd preferred the solitary sports. Back in school it had been track and field. As an adult he'd taken up cycling, kayaking, mountain climbing… The list went on and on.

When they'd broken up, the summer after graduation, he'd been sad, but not for long. He'd worked at a bike shop until he had enough cash for a trip to Europe. He'd always had a yearning to travel.

Meanwhile June had gone on to college, as she'd always planned, only now he knew that her first year would *not* have gone as planned, because she'd been pregnant. He'd had time to do some calculating and he figured the baby would have been born in March, at the latest.

Three months after she sent him a Christmas card saying everything was fine.

Another shadow passed by the window in the apartment. It seemed sad, somehow, that a new family had moved in, playing out their passions and dramas and dreams in the very rooms where June and Stephen had once lived.

Patrick glanced away. Nadine had removed her sunglasses—it was growing dark now—and was waiting for him patiently, though she was probably cold. Now that the sun was gone, the air was cooling rapidly.

"Thanks for waiting," he said, moving toward her.

"No problem. It must be quite a shock. Not only finding out you had a son. But he's eighteen years old."

"Yes. I cared about June, she was a good person and I don't want to blame her. But if she'd given me a chance, I would have liked to be a part of his life."

"Maybe the two of you would have gotten married."

Somehow he couldn't picture *that*. "Maybe."

They were at the café now, and he held the door open for Nadine. Inside, the room was welcoming, furnished with sofas and upholstered chairs, the windows draped in soft fabrics and the lighting warm and intimate. It felt a bit like walking into someone's home.

They were directed to a table for two next to a red-brick wall. Patrick helped Nadine off with her trench coat, then removed his leather jacket and hung both on a nearby coatrack.

He didn't normally pay much attention to the clothing people wore, but he did notice that Nadine's dress clung nicely to her petite figure. When she removed her hat, he saw that her thick, dark hair was pulled back in a simple ponytail. In his line of work, he saw women in practical ponytails all the time—but this one looked more elegant than sporty. The style showed off her delicate ears and earrings long enough to swing with each movement of her head.

He was reminded of how perfectly lovely she'd looked at the gala ball the other night. To the manner born, and all that stuff. He supposed being able to fit in with your surroundings was a useful talent when you were in her line of work.

He forced himself to wait until they'd both ordered coffee to ask, "So tell me what you've found out."

She cleared her throat. "I've contacted June's sister in Boston."

The obituary had mentioned Diane—whom he remembered vaguely.

"I tried to call Diane, too," he said. "But her number wasn't listed."

Nadine nodded, setting her earrings in motion again. "She still goes by Stone, though she is married. I hoped they might own a home and I was lucky. By checking the Boston property tax listings online I was able to find their address. From that, I figured out the most likely school for their children to attend."

That was clever. "But how did identifying the school help?"

"The school has a Web site. In one of the monthly newsletters, Diane was listed as pizza mom."

"Pizza mom. What in the world is that?"

"It sounds like a school fundraiser. The kids send in orders for a special pizza lunch once a month. At any rate, Diane was the volunteer organizer and her phone number was printed right next to her name."

Pretty ingenious legwork, Patrick thought, relieved to have this solid evidence that she knew what she was doing. "So you called her. Did you tell her I'd hired you to find Stephen?"

"Not exactly. I told her my name and that I lived in Manhattan. I said I had just heard that her sister had passed away and I was trying to find Stephen."

"You didn't mention me?"

"At this point I thought it would be good to say as little as possible. Diane made it very easy for me, actually. She didn't ask many questions at all. She's probably fielded a lot of calls since her sister passed away, so she just assumed I must be a friend."

He edged forward on his seat. "Did she tell you about Stephen? Is he living with her now? He's only eighteen."

Nadine sighed, which he didn't take as a good sign.

"Diane says that Stephen stayed with them for a few weeks after the funeral. But, apparently he wasn't very impressed with Boston. He decided to head to the Rocky Mountains, in Canada, with a friend. They're both certified ski instructors and they're hoping they can find a job."

"Canada? Hell, that's far." He'd been hoping to locate Stephen in Boston, just a short flight away. This was an unexpected complication, and disappointing. "Couldn't he find a job a little closer? There are plenty of ski hills in New England."

"Diane told me Stephen is taking his mother's death

pretty hard. He wanted to go somewhere far away, a place with no memories."

"He didn't have memories of his mother in Boston."

"Maybe Stephen craves adventure…like his father."

Her comment jolted Patrick. To this point his son had seemed more abstract than real. But he and Stephen shared the same DNA. And though it wasn't logical, he felt proud.

"Diane dropped Stephen off at the airport about two weeks ago," Nadine continued. "He and his friend were flying to Calgary, Alberta, where they planned to buy a cheap car, then head out to the Rockies."

"So now what?" Patrick wondered. Since finding out he had a son, he hadn't been able to sleep through the night once. He needed some resolution. Soon. "Canada is a big place. How do we find him?"

THE SERVER ARRIVED THEN TO SEE if they wanted to order anything to eat. Nadine could tell Patrick was impatient with the interruption, but she was suddenly starving.

She'd been working hard the past few days, running on adrenaline and nerves. She needed food to settle her stomach.

"I'll have the pasta special, please."

Patrick just shook his head. As soon as they were alone again, he asked, "So what's the plan?"

"We need to find where Stephen is working. It makes sense that he would head to one of the larger, world-class resorts, not just a local ski hill. I've done some research and it seems that there are three main possibilities, within two or three hours of Calgary."

"And they are?"

She pulled a sheet of paper from her bag and read out the list. "Sunshine Village at Banff, the Lake Louise ski hill or the Kicking Horse Resort in Golden."

"I've heard of all of those." His forehead knotted as he seemed to consider something. "In fact, I made some notes a few years ago when I was considering a book on ski adventures in the Canadian Rockies. And you're sure Stephen will be at one of those three places?"

"Pretty sure. The only other major ski hill in Canada is Whistler, but Stephen would have flown into Vancouver if he wanted to find a job at that resort."

True enough. "So what happens next? Have you tried phoning those resorts?"

"I've called, but so far I haven't had any luck. It turns out that they do a lot of hiring at the beginning of November. They won't have their full complement of employees entered into their systems for a few weeks yet."

"Hell." He shifted impatiently in his seat.

The server came with her dinner, and she picked up her fork. "Here's my recommendation. We wait fourteen days, and then I try calling the resorts again."

"That's too long," he said without even considering it. "You need to fly up there and look for him in person."

"Me? Fly to Canada?" Too late, Nadine realized she should have expected the suggestion. She could tell Patrick wasn't a patient man. And finding his son was clearly very important to him.

"I can't wait two more weeks to find him."

"We could hire an investigator in Calgary to follow this up," she suggested.

Patrick frowned. "I'm not keen on working with someone I haven't met with face-to-face."

She tried to think of a third option, but couldn't. Maybe she could dissuade him if she talked dollars. "It will be expensive. Air flights, hotels, rental cars. Plus I'd have to charge for meals, on top of my regular hourly fee."

"Obviously the retainer I paid you won't be nearly enough. I can write you another check right now." He pulled out a blank check from his wallet. She waited while he filled it out, then passed it to her.

Five thousand dollars. Holy crap. "This should cover it." She stared at the check, realizing she was out of excuses now. She had to take a trip to Canada—but how was she going to do that? She'd taken on this case intending to wrap it up while still carrying on with her usual receptionist duties.

Nadine swallowed. She'd have to think of something to tell the partners. "Right. Well, then. I guess I'm going to Canada."

Patrick rubbed his chin. "Maybe we should *both* go."

"Pardon me? But I thought you had a book due?"

"I can write just as well on the plane and in a hotel room in the Rockies as I can here in my apartment. If I travel with you, then I'll be right there to meet Stephen, as soon as you find him."

Oh, Lord, no. This job was going to be difficult enough, without having the client traveling with her— seeing all her mistakes firsthand.

"I'll call you as soon as I find him. You can catch the very next plane—"

"Calgary's on the other side of the continent. Even if I do manage to book the next available flight, I'll still lose a day to travel. And I know I'll be out of my mind with nerves the whole time. No. I really think this plan is the best. Besides, while I'm there, I can see if there's any potential for a book on the Canadian Rockies."

Nadine couldn't think of anything to say that would dissuade him.

With her head bowed over the dinner she no longer had any interest in eating, she tried to sneak a look at him. But she found him staring at *her*. His forehead was lined, his eyes appeared anxious. To her overwrought imagination, it seemed he was wondering if he'd made a mistake hiring her.

She wouldn't blame him, because she was wondering the same thing.

CHAPTER FIVE

THE NEXT MORNING, NADINE'S phone rang before it was
light. She pulled herself out of her warm bedding and
picked up the receiver she kept by her bed. Her mother
loved calling her early on the weekend.

"Hi, Mom."

"Ahh—this is Patrick O'Neil. I was trying to reach
Nadine Kimble."

Adrenaline pumped through her, waking her more
effectively than any alarm clock. "This is Nadine."

She swung her feet to the wool rug, still holding the
receiver to her ear.

Patrick O'Neil. She'd given him her home number
last night so he could call after he'd made their travel
arrangements. But she hadn't expected to hear from him
this early. According to the digital display on the built-
in media center across the room, it wasn't even eight.

"I managed to get two tickets on a ten o'clock flight.
I hope that leaves you enough time to pack."

"Ten o'clock this evening? It'll be tight, but I should
be able to manage."

"Ten o'clock this *morning.*"

Good Lord. Was he serious?

"I can arrange for a limo to pick you up in an hour.
Is that enough time?"

"You're kidding, right?"

He was silent for a bit, then said, "I thought we agreed I would go for the first *available* flight?"

"Yes. But—"

"As long as you have your credit card and your passport, you'll be fine."

Holy crap. Adrenaline surging, Nadine ran to the bathroom and checked her hair. It needed washing, but she would never have time to dry it properly. She tried to remember where she'd put her passport after her last international trip to…

She thought it had been Belize. But it might have been that shopping trip to Paris.

"You really don't waste time, do you?" she said, switching the phone to Speaker so she could squeeze toothpaste on her brush.

"I figured the faster we got on this the better."

Sure. But giving her one hour notice? She started thinking of all the things she would need. A trip to Canada meant warm coats, boots and bulky sweaters.

"Oh, and try to limit your luggage to carry-on. We have to make a connection in Toronto and the timing is kind of tight."

Hell.

"I have everything organized. All I need from you is your address."

So he could pick her up in the limo. Only, she couldn't let him do that. Her Upper East Side address would be sure to lead to questions she didn't want to answer.

"I need to get my files from the office. How about you pick me up there?"

Thinking of all she had to do, in one short hour, made Nadine's stomach swirl.

Find her ID, pack her bag, cancel Sunday dinner with her parents, let the people at the office know she was going away for a few days....

Oh, boy. That was going to be the hardest. Maybe she should just phone the office number and leave a message. But that would give Lindsay and Nathan zero notice that she wasn't going to be at work on Monday.

After a quick shower, Nadine dressed in airplane clothes—no metal zippers, or belts, shoes that slipped off easily, layers in case the plane was too hot or too cold.

Who should she call—Nathan or Lindsay? She would feel extra guilty lying to Nathan, he was such a straight arrow himself. But Lindsay would give her a grilling, and she didn't have time to come up with a great cover story.

In the end, she dialed the number for Nathan's cell phone, because she was certain that he would accept her "need to go away for a few days on a personal matter" without any questions.

As she waited for him to answer—or, better yet, to be diverted to his message service—she started searching through her underwear drawer for her passport.

While she was there, she might as well pack her underwear, too.

Suddenly she heard Lindsay speaking. "Fox here."

"Oh, hi, Lindsay. I thought I was calling Nathan."

"He's in the shower. What's up?"

Nadine drew a deep breath and stopped looking for the passport. She needed one hundred percent concentration now.

"I was just calling to let you know that I have to go out of town on a personal matter. I'm not going to be able to make it into work on Monday or Tuesday. Wednesday might be iffy, too."

"Wow. That personal matter sure came up quickly. You didn't say anything about this yesterday."

"I'm very sorry for the late notice."

"Not a problem. Actually, it's a good time for you to take some holidays as you won't get many opportunities once Kate is on maternity leave."

"Right. Well, I guess I'd better get going…"

"Where?"

Nadine had been hoping to hang up, but Lindsay spoke too quickly. "It's—nowhere special."

"Your voice sounds strange."

Oh, she'd *known* Lindsay would give her a grilling.

"Does this have something to do with that man you were texting at work the other day?"

Nadine almost laughed with relief. Finally a question she could answer without lying. "Yes."

"Well. That's moving fast, isn't it?"

Nadine had to admit that it was.

"I'm sure you know what you're doing," Lindsay said. "But be careful. You can't always take people at face value."

As she was finally able to hang up the phone, Nadine thought that Lindsay didn't know just how right she was.

NADINE WISHED HER FATHER could see how economically she'd packed for the trip to Canada. He would have been proud.

She'd limited herself to one jacket—the Versace convertible down ski jacket she'd worn on the family's last trip to the Swiss Alps. She'd be wearing that on the plane, of course. In her leather carry-on she'd managed to compress black ski pants and trousers, several turtlenecks—which were warm but didn't take up as much room as a sweater—and just one dress, which she could vary with an assortment of tights, scarves and jewelry.

In her briefcase she packed her laptop, phone, camera and the file of notes she'd accumulated so far. She was seriously tempted to also pack her copy of *The Complete Idiot's Guide to Private Investigating*. But that would be a dead giveaway if Patrick happened to see it.

Finally, she locked up her apartment and took a taxi across the park. She arrived at the office two minutes before the limo. Her father would probably have been more amazed than proud.

Patrick didn't seem impressed with her accomplishment, though. She supposed he got ready for trips at a moment's notice all the time. He gave her a casual hello as he climbed out of the backseat, then took her bag.

"Thanks. Be careful. It's heavier than it looks."

He raised one eyebrow at her, then picked it up as if it was filled with down feathers. He set it into the trunk next to his carry-on bag which looked beaten—if not tortured.

"I guess you travel a lot," she said once they were in the car, heading for LaGuardia. She'd visited many countries with her family, but she imagined her parents' idea of a vacation differed significantly from the kind of trips Patrick made.

"It's my job to travel. It's been my job for almost twenty years."

"Do you ever get tired of being on the road all the time?"

"I've never thought about it, so I guess not."

His expression was grim as he turned his gaze to the street ahead of them. She got the feeling that he would have been more comfortable driving than being the passenger.

She felt uneasy sitting next to him, and wished again that she could have gone on this trip without him. He was far too observant for her liking. She would have to be on her guard every instant of every day.

Soon they were dropped off at the airport, and since Patrick had their boarding cards downloaded to his BlackBerry, they just had to clear customs then go to the gate. She didn't realize until they were being seated that they were traveling executive class.

"How nice," she said, taking the window seat and stowing her briefcase under the chair in front of her. "I guess when you fly as often as you do, you deserve the little luxuries."

"I almost always fly economy," he corrected her. "But when I ask someone to leave their home to take care of my personal business, then I figure I owe them the courtesy of making the trip as comfortable as I can."

"Well, I am comfortable. So thank you."

"Good." He leaned back into his seat and let out a long sigh. Then he turned to her. "I'm sorry if I've been a little tense this morning. I'm unbelievably nervous."

"That's totally understandable."

"I can't believe I'm about to meet my son. It could even happen tonight."

Nadine felt obliged to lower his expectations. "But it probably *won't* be tonight. We have *three* resorts to check, and no guarantee that he hasn't changed his mind about working in Canada for the winter. For all we know, he met someone who suggested they apply for a job at Club Med so they could spend the winter on the beach."

"Good God." Patrick sounded appalled by that.

"There's something else you need to prepare yourself for," she added. "We won't know for certain that Stephen Stone is your son until we get the results from a DNA test."

He frowned. "Who said anything about DNA testing?"

"It's standard procedure in a case like this," she assured him.

He shook his head firmly. "If there was any chance at all that Stephen wasn't my son, June wouldn't have written that letter."

"You trust her that much?"

"I do."

How very strange, Nadine realized. *I'm actually feeling a little jealous of this June.* "You must have loved her very much."

"I loved her," he agreed.

She waited for him to say more and, when he didn't, sighed with frustration. Then she immediately chided herself.

Lindsay had talked to her, over and over, about the importance of not getting emotionally involved in a case. And here she was suffering some sort of mild crush on her very first client.

But that aside, she had to deal with his expectations about this boy. She figured he would probably be willing to offer financial assistance to Stephen even if he wasn't his biological son.

"I don't want to insult June. You obviously thought very highly of her. But you're paying me to be objective. It strikes me as possible that she might have seen that you'd enjoyed a degree of success, and if she was worried about her son's future, she might be tempted to capitalize on a past friendship."

"But that's the whole point. We *were* friends. All she would have had to do is ask. Preferably before she died."

"Maybe she felt too many years had drifted by with no contact."

"She has only herself to blame for that. Those Christmas cards were the only time I heard from her."

"Maybe she needed to move on. Or maybe she was worried you would find out about your son."

"Yeah. She seemed pretty determined to keep that secret. I suppose I should feel grateful that she allowed me to pursue my dream career. But somehow all I feel is resentment."

"It's only natural that you'd wonder about the road not taken. You know…a wife and kids…"

"…and a beautiful home in Brooklyn Heights? Not my dream. At least it never was." He turned to look at her in that special way of his that made her feel as if he was seeing her inner thoughts.

"Is personal counseling included with your fees?" he asked.

She felt herself blush. "Sorry. I should mind my own business, huh?"

"I have a feeling that's something you wouldn't be very good at. And I'm not suggesting that's bad. It's probably your curiosity about people that led you to this career."

His smile changed, shifted into something intimate. She swallowed and realized she was breaking Lindsay's rule again. No emotions. No personal involvement.

Heavens, this was so much harder than she'd expected.

PATRICK THOUGHT THE P.I. HE'D hired was the most feminine woman he'd ever met. Maybe it was because he was used to being with women who had similar interests to him. Women who enjoyed extreme sports, who climbed mountains, who skied out-of-bounds searching for that perfect, untouched bowl of powder.

The women he knew, the women he dated, had rough hands and sun-beaten skin—like him. They didn't wear heels because they were too impractical. The same went for makeup and perfume. They dressed in Dri-Fit because it was comfortable and fleece because it was warm.

They talked about their sports, and the weather, their training regimes and…all too often…their injuries.

Nadine was nothing like those women and definitely not his type. But she kept drawing his eye and making him smile.

He couldn't believe how slender her fingers were, or how gracefully her hands moved when she talked. Her teeth were perfectly white, and her eyelashes curled in the most adorable way.

And the way she dressed…

A few times when he'd been flicking through channels on TV, he watched bits of *Sex and the City*. He'd never met anyone who dressed like those women, until Nadine. Just look at what she had on for this trip. Fur-lined boots with heels, jeans so blue he'd swear they'd never been washed, and a ski jacket that looked way better than any ski jacket he'd ever seen before.

Every detail about her fascinated him, and he had to keep reminding himself that she was a legitimate P.I., a woman with her feet on the ground, who worked hard for her living. A woman who deserved his professional respect, not his secret, lustful desire.

In Toronto they changed planes and once again they were seated in executive class, with Nadine by the window. For this longer leg of their trip, he pulled out his laptop and started organizing his notes for the revisions.

Nadine opened her laptop, too. He noticed she was making case notes—*his* case notes—and he was tempted to ask if he could read them.

Then she switched documents and a map popped on the screen. He leaned over for a look, but a whiff of her softly sweet perfume momentarily distracted him. Damn, she smelled good.

"We'll go to Sunshine first," she said, clearly thinking he was looking at the map. "It's about a two-hour drive from the airport."

"We don't have any rooms booked," he realized belatedly.

"Don't worry. The season hasn't really kicked off yet. We shouldn't have a problem getting something. They have units right on the ski hill. That's probably the smartest place to stay, though we will need to leave the car in the parking lot and take a gondola."

"How long do you think you'll need in each place?"

"One day, tops. Maybe less."

"Okay. Should be a short trip, then."

"Really short if we get lucky and find Stephen at the

first ski hill." She smiled at him hopefully, and he actually got the sensation of something fluttering in his gut.

Was it nerves about the possibility that he might meet his son as early as tomorrow?

Or was it excitement at the idea of spending the next few days with this intriguing woman?

JUST BEFORE LANDING, the pilot came on the intercom to tell them it was snowing in Calgary. A chorus of groans rose up from the passengers. Nadine wondered anxiously about the roads.

Sure enough, once they'd deplaned and picked up the Subaru Patrick had reserved for their trip, visibility was getting to be an issue.

"I've driven in worse than this," Patrick assured her, but as they left the city lights behind, Nadine was spooked by the utter darkness around her. It was only six-thirty, but at this time of year, this far north, the sun was long gone.

"I never thought I'd say this, but I wouldn't mind a few streetlamps and neon signs."

"You're in the foothills of the Rocky Mountains, sweetheart, and those words are blasphemy here."

Maybe so, but between the blackness of the night and the hypnotic pummeling of snowflakes, there were times she couldn't see the lines on the highway. Meanwhile cars were still traveling at speeds exceeding the posted 110 kilometers per hour limit.

She glanced sideways at Patrick. Though she could only see his profile, he seemed calm. She watched his hands on the wheel and thought how capable they appeared. And suddenly she wasn't nervous anymore. Not about the roads, anyway.

"Would you like music?"

They discovered they both enjoyed jazz and she found a public radio station that was playing something by Diana Krall. She didn't know the name of the song, but she would recognize that smooth contralto anywhere.

The atmosphere in the car was cozy and warm. Nadine reclined comfortably and glanced again at Patrick. He seemed as at home here as he had in New York City. She suspected he was that sort of man—able to fit in wherever he went.

She did feel safe with him, though. In a physical sense, anyway. On another level, she knew she could never completely let down her guard around him. This was a work assignment, and if she wanted to be a professional, she had to remember to be sharp and observant at all times.

Another one of Lindsay and Nathan's lessons.

Still, there wasn't much to observe in the car. Other than Patrick.

"Did you grow up in Manhattan?"

He shifted slightly in his seat, as if her words had interrupted his inner musings. "No. Upper State."

"In one of those lovely little towns with a pretty white church and houses with picket fences and friendly neighbors?" She had an idealized conception of small-town living, she knew, based on shows like the *Gilmore Girls*.

"Some of the houses had picket fences. Not ours, though."

She wondered if she imagined his tone had turned grim. "Did you have brothers and sisters?"

"Nope. Just me and my mom." He turned for a brief look at her. "My dad split when I was real young."

"I'm sorry. Did you still see him?"

"He moved to Boston, got a better job and a younger wife. They had two kids of their own and whenever I went to visit, that three-thousand square foot home of theirs felt mighty small. So gradually more and more time began lapsing between my invitations to visit."

On his behalf she resented that word *invitation*. A child shouldn't have to wait to be invited to spend time with his father. "Were you close to your mom?"

"Very. Which made it all the harder to see how she lived, compared to Dad's new wife. Mom worked two jobs, volunteered at my school, grew all our vegetables in a plot she rented from a neighbor. I never saw her relaxing, she claimed she didn't know how."

"That doesn't seem fair."

"One of Mom's favorite sayings was that you should hope for fairness, but when it doesn't happen, be prepared to fight. We didn't have much money, but she always found enough for us to have fun. It's thanks to my mom's sacrifices that I learned to ski."

"You're speaking about her in the past tense."

"She passed away several years ago."

"And you still miss her."

"Sure. She was my only family."

No mention of his father, she noticed.

"If I have a regret, it's that my book sales were just starting to take off when my mother got sick. If she could have lived another year, I might have been able to do something nice for her. Maybe even buy her a house."

"Seeing you happy and successful was probably all she really cared about." She hesitated, knowing she shouldn't probe, but in the end couldn't help herself. "How about your father? Is he still alive?"

Patrick's mouth hardened again. "Yeah. He sent flowers to Mom's funeral. Big deal, huh? I phoned him later and asked why he bothered when he hadn't helped her any when she was alive. We haven't spoken since."

Suddenly Nadine had a little more appreciation for why he resented not being told about his son. His father had been largely absent from his life. Now, inadvertently, he'd done the same to his own child.

"I'm prepared for Stephen to be angry," he said, as if he knew exactly what she was thinking. "Even though I had no way of knowing he existed, from his point of view, I was an absent father. I know how that hurts when you're a kid."

"I wonder why June made the choice that she did?"

"Yeah. I wish I'd had a chance to ask her that question in person. I'm guessing she came to regret her decision later. That's probably why she chose to tell me the news in a letter after her death, rather than when she was still alive."

In a way it had been a cowardly choice. But who was she to judge? Her life, by almost all standards, had been privileged, easy, happy. She'd had no difficult choices to make, no defining moments that tested her wisdom and courage.

"What about you, Nadine? Are your parents still together?"

Nadine tensed. That was the danger in asking about his life. She had to be prepared for him to ask the same questions of her. She thought carefully before answering. "I couldn't imagine them without one another. They're definitely a matched set."

"Well, you're lucky then."

"Yes." In many, many ways she'd been born lucky. And yet with that she carried this mantle of guilt. Why should she have so much, and others so little? She hadn't earned any of her family's money herself. Yet, she enjoyed all the benefits. The imbalance had never sat right with her.

"I want to work," she'd told her parents when she finished university. "In a real job. I want to be hired for myself, not because I'm a Waverly."

They couldn't understand her thinking. When she did manage to find a job working for Lindsay, they thought she was only doing it to hurt them.

"Any siblings?"

"I'm an only child, too."

Patrick slowed. They were nearing the gates to Banff National Park. He'd brought a GPS with him, and Nadine checked the remaining time for their trip. One more hour to go.

What would they find when they arrived at Sunshine Village?

Her stomach tightened. Would Patrick's son be there?

CHAPTER SIX

THE NEXT MORNING, NADINE stretched in her king-size bed. She was in a cozily decorated room at the Mountain Lodge at Sunshine Village and bright light streamed in from a window that overlooked the main ski hill.

As she thought about the day ahead, she started to feel uncomfortably nervous. Last night she and Patrick had agreed that they would both do their own things today—he would write, she would try to find his son. Then, at three o'clock, they would meet up at the Lookout Bistro.

Nadine had decided that she would check with administration first. Too nervous to eat anything, she dressed quickly, then went in search of the human relations department. She found the office in a state of chaos. Lots of young people were lined up, filling out forms, asking questions.

Finally she was able to talk to someone in charge, a blonde woman with a short, sporty hairdo and a propensity to speak very quickly.

"How can I help you?"

Nadine could tell her mind was on approximately a hundred other matters of pressing importance. She passed her a business card. "My name is Nadine Kimble. I'm trying to find a young man, Stephen Stone, on behalf of his family. We understood that he might be applying for a job here."

"Him and a thousand other kids. As you can see, November is when we do most of our hiring. Now, if you could come back in three weeks, it would be a lot easier for me to give you a definite answer."

"I traveled from New York City. Is there any way you could help me now?"

"Well, I can check if he's on payroll. But even if he isn't that's no guarantee. As you can see—" she indicated stacks of paper on her desk "—I have a lot of unprocessed paperwork here."

Nadine murmured with sympathy. "I couldn't have come at a worse time, could I? Still, if you would check that payroll, I would be very grateful."

The woman nodded curtly, then turned to her computer. Nadine glanced around the room as she waited. Most of the kids in the room seemed to be in their late teens or early twenties. Boys outnumbered girls by a ratio of at least four to one. Listening to them speaking, she caught a number of Australian and New Zealand accents.

Suddenly it hit her that she'd made a mistake. A big one.

She'd come all this way without any idea what Stephen Stone looked like. He could be standing in this room with her right now, and she wouldn't even know it.

Damn it, what a juvenile error.

She'd been so keen to impress the partners with what a terrific investigator she could be. She'd been so sure they were wrong when they said she wasn't ready.

But they'd been right. She tried to wipe the look of

panic from her face as the HR woman looked up from her computer.

"I'm sorry, but we have no one with a last name of Stone on our payroll. Why don't you call again in a few weeks, in case his application is still in process?"

She handed Nadine a card, which she pocketed with a faint thank-you.

God, she had screwed this up so badly. And Patrick had already spent so much money, flying them up here, renting a car, covering their rooms. Did she dare admit to him what she'd done?

Nadine trudged over to the Day Lodge. Since it was a Sunday, there were quite a few skiers milling around, having a quick bite to eat before hitting the hills and making the most of the early snow.

Nadine ordered a hot chocolate, then went to sit at one of the tables by a window. The mountains looked stunning against the backdrop of a perfect blue sky, but her mood only sank lower at the amazing beauty.

She had no right putting her ambitions ahead of the needs of a client. Patrick O'Neil had come to The Fox & Fisher Detective Agency because he'd heard it was a reputable firm, known for providing quick results. And here she was, wasting his time and money, botching a job that Kate, Lindsay or Nathan would have found easy.

Nadine sipped her drink until the cup was empty, idly watching the skiers outside, while she beat herself up for her incompetence.

After fifteen minutes, her mood shifted.

Well, maybe she'd made a mistake not finding a photograph, but she was here now. She might as well do her best anyway.

She decided that she would talk to as many people as possible. And the best way to do that, would be to put on a set of skis herself, and get out there.

Mind made up, Nadine bought herself a day pass—remembering to question the attendant about Stephen—then went to the main rental shop. She joined a queue, filled out the forms that asked for information about her height, weight and level of ski ability. Eventually it was her turn, and a polite young man wearing a warm hoodie over ski pants, helped her pick out boots, poles and skis.

"Do you happen to know a guy named Stephen Stone?" she asked as she struggled with the fastening on the first ski boot. "He's eighteen years old. A few weeks ago he and a buddy headed this way looking for a job as a ski instructor."

He bent over to help her, easily snapping the clasp closed. "Can't say that I do," he said. "How does that feel?"

She stood up, wiggled her toes, and immediately missed the custom-fitted boots in her winter closet at home. "Fine."

"Good. We'll adjust your bindings, then you'll be ready to go." He helped her remove the boot, then took it to a counter where another young man was laying out the skis. "Frank, do you know someone named Stephen Stone?"

"Maybe he goes by Steve," Nadine added hopefully.

The kid named Frank cast his eyes up thoughtfully for a second, then shook his head. "Nope."

Ten minutes later, Nadine was no wiser, but outfitted to hit the slopes.

At every chair and T-bar lift, she asked the attendants

about Stephen. When someone from the ski guard happened by, she stopped and asked the same question.

After three runs up and down the mountain, she felt as if she'd spoken to everyone on the hill. She was also getting hungry.

She rode the lifts to the top of the mountain again, and went in to Goat's Eye Gardens—a cute bistro with a marvelous view over the mountain range. She would really enjoy a burger and a Coke about now.

Thanks to the sunshine and the sweat she'd worked up on the mountain, it was warm enough to eat outside, and she went to the patio to enjoy al fresco dining.

A couple of kids with badges identifying them as ski instructors happened to be out there, too. At this point, she was resigned to failure, but still, when one of them smiled at her, she smiled back.

"Can I ask you something?"

"Sure."

"I'm wondering if you've heard of someone named Stephen Stone. He was supposed to be heading this way, looking for a job as a ski instructor."

"Yeah? You know, that name sounds familiar. Scott?"

The other instructor lifted his goggles, revealing warm, brown eyes. "That's the redhead from New York City." He looked at Nadine. "He had the same accent as you. Sort of. We talked to him at the bar last weekend."

Nadine almost choked with excitement. "Is he here? Did he get a job?"

Scott shook his head. "I don't think so. All the instructor positions were already filled. I told him he should try Kicking Horse. They don't start their season as early as we do."

WHEN PATRICK SAW ALL the fresh powder on the hills, it almost killed him to close the curtains and start writing. But he did it. His deadline hovered too close for him to goof off now.

He ordered room service for breakfast and room service for lunch. It was one o'clock when he reached his target for the day, and he closed down his computer with relief.

The mountains were calling. He only had time for a few runs before his meeting with Nadine, but he couldn't resist.

He dressed in his ski pants and jacket, then went out to buy a half-day pass and rent some equipment. When he told the guys behind the counter some of the best places he'd skied, they were impressed.

"Man, you better check out the back of Goat's Eye."

"Thanks." Patrick studied a map of the ski hill for a bit, then headed for the quad chair. There wasn't any line up and he had the four-seater bench to himself on the ride up the mountain.

Idly he watched the skiers below him, as he wondered about Nadine. Where was she? He'd hoped she would call with news about Stephen, but his cell phone hadn't rung even once. Meanwhile, as the chair climbed inexorably up the mountain, the views became increasingly impressive.

Patrick felt his worries—about Stephen, about the deadline—drop away with each foot of elevation gained. Something about being in the mountains always brought him to a place of mental clarity and emotional peace.

When he finally reached the top, he surveyed the

panorama with intense anticipation. One, two, three, he counted in his head, then zoom—he pushed off and let his body take over. Down the slope, then a turn to the right, then the left, until he hit moguls and began carving his way through them. The sound of his skis on the snow filled his ears, and his body fell into a natural, joyous rhythm.

There were only a few other brave souls on this side of the mountain, probably because it was so early in the season. He had to avoid a few bare patches, but on the whole the conditions were great.

There was a steep elevation drop and suddenly he could see that the path ahead split in two around a stand of evergreen trees. He was about to veer to the left, when he noticed a familiar-looking jacket to the right.

Nadine's ski jacket was that same shade of green.

He turned right.

She had several hundred yards on him, but gradually he gained on her. Her form was tight and controlled, and he wondered where the hell she had learned to ski like that.

At one point he stopped, just to allow himself time to watch her. He realized he was smiling. There was something so damn light and graceful about her. Her movements, the wide sweeping arcs of her skis, reminded him of seagulls coasting on a summer breeze.

By now, she'd gained a lot of ground on him and he pushed off, pointing his skis straight down the hill. The speed was a rush, but eventually he cut a short turn to the right, then another in the opposite direction, still keeping back far enough that she didn't notice him.

The trail veered again, this time giving them the option to tackle a steep slope of moguls or a pleasant-looking intermediate run.

Patrick expected Nadine to head for the intermediate run, but she surprised him. She picked off the moguls with amazing skill and he kept a safe distance behind her, getting as much pleasure from her finesse as he did from his own.

Finally the trail leveled off on an easy descent to the main lodge. Patrick paused to check his watch and was surprised to see it was already quarter to three. He skied up beside her, then raised his goggles. The sunlight radiating off all that white snow was almost blinding.

"Hey there! Nice skiing!"

"Patrick." Though he'd surprised her, she didn't falter on her skis. "I was just heading in for our meeting."

Patrick considered suggesting they take another run first. But now that he was back on level ground, his real-life worries returned, too. He wanted to know if she had any news about his son.

"Let's drop off our equipment," he suggested. "And then we can talk."

PATRICK DISPLAYED IMPRESSIVE patience, not asking Nadine what she'd discovered until they were seated in the Lookout Bistro and had ordered drinks and munchies.

Nadine was feeling better about her assignment, hopeful that she could still get the results Patrick wanted and report back to the others without too much egg on her face.

Running into those ski instructors on the top of the mountain had been her first lucky break.

"I'm afraid Stephen isn't working here," she said

without preamble. "But the good news is that I found some guys who met him in the bar last weekend. They advised him to try Kicking Horse. They said that was the best option for skiing instructor jobs at this point in the season."

Patrick rubbed his jaw as he absorbed her news. "I guess it was too much to hope we'd find him the first place we looked."

"At least we know he was here. And, something else. The guys mentioned that Stephen had red hair." It wasn't as helpful as a photograph. But red hair was unusual enough that it would be noticed. And, hopefully, remembered.

"Is that right?" Patrick looked down at his hands resting on the scarred wooden table. "When I was a kid, I had red hair, too. It got darker as I grew older."

It was a significant point of similarity, Nadine thought. But still not absolute proof that Stephen truly was Patrick's biological son.

"Good work, Nadine," Patrick said. "It feels good to know we're getting closer."

Nadine basked in his praise. She'd been too hard on herself this morning. She was doing fine here. She really was.

The server arrived with their drinks and food. Nadine was famished.

"It's amazing what a great appetite you get after some exercise and fresh air," she commented as she reached for another sweet-potato fry.

"I couldn't agree more. By the way, where did you learn to ski like that? I don't know anyone who grew up in New York City who skis like you."

"Stephen grew up there and he became an instructor," she pointed out. "As for me, my parents love two sports—tennis and skiing. We spent most of our family vacations doing one or the other."

"You have to be a good skier to master the icy slopes of the hills in New England," Patrick allowed.

Nadine nodded, not about to tell him that she'd actually honed her skills in the top resorts in the world. Her dad loved Jackson Hole, her Mom preferred Gstaad, Switzerland.

She finished drinking her cola. "I guess we should pack up and get moving. According to those guys I was talking to, it's about two hours to Kicking Horse from here. Apparently the terrain gets rough. The highway is only two lanes and the road has a lot of deep bends and twists."

Patrick checked his watch. "The sun will be setting in about an hour and a half. We'll have to do at least part of the drive in the dark. But at least the forecast isn't calling for more snow tonight."

PATRICK OFFERED TO DRIVE AGAIN, which was fine with Nadine. She settled into the passenger seat of the Subaru with the two take-out coffees they'd bought after disembarking from the gondola. After fitting the cups into the holders by the gearshift, she did up her seat belt.

The trip started out well. The sun was already behind the mountains, but it wasn't yet dark and the roads had been plowed clean after last night's storm.

She was feeling a lot better now than she had this morning. She felt she was making good progress finding Stephen. She even doubted if any of the others could have done any better.

The skiing had helped improve her mood, too. There was nothing like a day spent in the mountains. She was kind of flattered that Patrick had been so impressed with her skill level. It felt good to see the approval in his eyes when he looked at her.

Of course, he was an amazing skier, too. She hadn't had as much opportunity to observe him on the hill, but from what she'd seen, he'd moved as if his skis were a natural extension of his body.

Right now, he was focused on the road, allowing her plenty of opportunity to study him. She liked that his features were a little rugged and that his hair was such an interesting combination of golden brown and dark red. He had nice eyes, too, eyes that seemed to say more than he ever did.

He liked to ask questions more than answer them, she'd noticed. But they had a long drive ahead of them. Maybe she could get him talking.

It would be a good test, she decided. One of an investigator's most important skills was the ability to extract information from other people.

She popped the lid on her coffee and took a sip. Then she asked him how his writing had gone.

"Really well. I just need to stay disciplined about it and I shouldn't have any trouble meeting my deadline."

"Do you ever think you'll write something besides a travel book?"

He seemed surprised by the question. "I've never thought about it."

"Tell me why you love to travel so much."

He glanced at her, amused. "You're full of questions today."

"Well, we have a long drive ahead of us. I thought we could chat. Or would you rather listen to the radio?"

"I don't think we'll have very good reception. I don't mind talking. I think I like traveling because I didn't get to do much of it as a kid."

"Lots of children don't get to travel much. They don't all become adventure travel writers."

"True enough. I guess I was always a person who was looking for the road less traveled. Give me option a, b or c, and I'll always pick d."

She smiled. Yes. She hadn't known him very long, but she could tell that was an accurate description.

She asked him about the various places he'd traveled, and Patrick seemed happy to tell her about them. He talked as they drove the forty-five minutes to Lake Louise, then the extra half hour to a small town called Field. According to the GPS, they had about an hour left to reach Golden.

The light had faded now, and Patrick started using his high beams whenever there was no opposing traffic— which was fairly often.

Though the car was warm, Nadine shivered. "It's awfully dark and deserted out here."

No sooner had she said that, than she heard the rumble of thunder. "Is that a storm?"

The rumble grew louder and puffs of snow came flying at the windshield. Patrick glanced at the rearview mirror, then hit the brakes. The car slowed quickly, as a wall of snow suddenly appeared on the highway, just visible within the range of the halogen high beams.

"It's an avalanche," Nadine said quietly, shock making her brain numb.

CHAPTER SEVEN

"THAT WAS AN AVALANCHE, all right." Patrick jerked the car into Reverse and backed up about twenty feet. Snow, as deep as the car, blocked the road in front of them.

"We just missed being buried alive." Nadine shivered as the shock started to wear off.

"And we're not hanging around to see if there's more coming."

Tires squealing, Patrick executed a three-point turn, then started back in the direction they'd just come from.

Nadine sat tensely. Though it was quiet now, in her mind she could still hear the ominous rumbling sound of the avalanche.

Patrick glanced in the rearview mirror. "I sure hope no one was caught in that. We should report this as soon as possible."

Nadine tried her cell phone but wasn't surprised that the area had no service. "If we'd left the hotel one minute earlier, we would have been—"

She stopped. It was unbearable to imagine what it would have been like to be swallowed up by all of that snow, packed in so tightly it would be impossible to open the car door, or even escape through a window....

"Don't think about it." Patrick reached over and touched her hand. "We're safe. That's all that counts."

He was right, but she still couldn't stop shaking. She'd seen signs on the highway that said Don't Stop, Avalanche Area. But she'd figured they were like those warnings to watch out for deer that were never there.

"Don't think about what *might* have happened," Patrick cautioned again. "That's a game that will paralyze you with fear if you play it too often. What we need is a backup plan. Do you recall seeing any motels along this road?"

"There wasn't much after Field. Wait a minute." There had been something... "I did notice a sign to Emerald Lake Lodge. Let me check the GPS, see if it's working." She held it close to the window and was grateful when it was able to pick up a satellite reading.

"Emerald Lake Lodge is twenty minutes away," she said.

"Let's do it."

PATRICK WASN'T EXPECTING much on this godforsaken stretch of highway, but Emerald Lake Lodge turned out to be a hidden treasure. They had to leave the car in a parking lot, then were ferried by a small bus across a tiny bridge to a cluster of buildings including a rustic lodge and about a dozen smaller chalets. The rooflines of the lodge were outlined in sparkling lights and in the air was the welcoming scent of burning hickory.

"It appears we've lucked out," Nadine commented.

"Treat yourself to dinner in the main dining room and you'll really feel pampered," their driver told them. He stopped by the side of the lodge. "Once you've checked into your rooms, we'll bring up your luggage. It'll probably be waiting by the time you arrive."

A warm fire greeted them in the main lobby, along with the aroma of gourmet food from the adjoining dining area. On the other side of the lobby was a casual lounge for drinks or lighter fare. Directly ahead was a curving staircase leading to unknown areas.

One of two young women behind a counter waved at them to step forward.

"We need two rooms," Patrick explained. "We were stopped by an avalanche on the highway about twenty minutes west from here."

The young woman nodded at her coworker. "Denise, you'd better call Avalanche Control and report that."

Denise nodded and picked up the phone.

"That must have given you a scare."

Patrick noticed the name tag discreetly pinned to her lapel. "It sure did, Andie. But fortunately we weren't injured. I hope no one else was, either. Traffic was pretty light."

"It's low season, which is lucky for you, as we have several vacancies. You said you wanted two rooms? Would you like them side by side?"

Patrick glanced at Nadine, who nodded. "That sounds fine."

He caught her eye, and she smiled, and suddenly he was wishing they were here under an entirely different scenario. Because the truth was, he didn't want separate rooms, at all.

Nadine turned away, seemingly fascinated by a flower arrangement on the counter. But he could see the pink rising on her cheeks.

Andie pulled out a map of the property and showed them how to reach their chalet. "You're staying right across from the outdoor hot tub. It's a favorite among our guests. And would you like me to make you a reservation for dinner?"

Again Patrick checked with Nadine and when she nodded, he said, "Sure, that would be great." He took the keys and passed one to her. She accepted it, careful not to meet his gaze this time.

They went outside, boots crunching on snow, breath forming clouds of crystals that hung in the still air. The chalets were connected by paths wide enough to allow for the passage of the golf-cart–size vehicles that were used by the staff to transport luggage and supplies.

"I'm glad they don't allow cars in here," Nadine said. "This place has a lovely, European atmosphere don't you think? It's like a charming Swiss village."

"Have you been to Switzerland?" She'd asked so many questions about his travels that he'd assumed she hadn't seen much of the world.

She seemed to lose her footing, and he took her arm, amazed at how delicate she was, how much he liked holding her.

"Sorry," she said. "I slipped on a patch of ice. Oh, look. That must be the hot tub." She pointed to an area to their right. He couldn't see much, other than a large cloud of steam. But he could hear the quiet murmur of conversation, then a woman's laugh.

Their chalets were to the left. Patrick waited until Nadine was safely inside her room before he unlocked his own. The room was decorated in mountain lodge style, with furniture fashioned from logs and two willow chairs nestled in front of a wood-burning fireplace.

The furniture looked rustic, but when he tested the

bed, it was extremely comfortable, with soft white linens and a feather duvet.

He'd sleep well here tonight. As long as he could forget that tomorrow he might meet his son.

As long as he could stop thinking about the woman who would be sleeping next door.

NADINE WORE HER DRESS to dinner. She covered her bare shoulders with one of the scarves she'd brought with her. It was black with silver and gold threads that caught the light from the candles and made it dance.

Patrick had ordered wine. And they'd both decided to try the evening special, which was venison served with a cranberry hazelnut risotto.

Nadine smoothed the white linen tablecloth with her hand. "I can't believe a place like this can exist here…in the middle of nowhere."

"Apparently the lake is that way." Patrick indicated a direction beyond the lodge. "It's reputed to be one of the most beautiful lakes in the world."

"Maybe you'll have to write about this place in one of your travel books."

He nodded. "Between heli-skiing, white-water rafting and mountain climbing, I think I'm going to find enough to interest my usual audience."

She leaned closer to him. "Do you try all the activities you write about in your books?"

"Yes. All of them." His gaze seemed to dip a little. From her face to the low neckline of her dress.

Instinctively she pulled her scarf tight to her body, even as an unaccustomed heat washed over her.

There'd been men in her past. Lots of duty dates arranged by her parents and a few romantic relationships with boys from school and university. But there was no one from her past who could compare to Patrick O'Neil.

At some point on this trip...she couldn't quite pinpoint the exact moment...she had started developing an attraction to this man. More than attraction, actually, because she'd felt that from their first meeting.

No, this was more like a magnetic pull. And she was almost positive the feeling was mutual.

She wasn't too sure what a worldly, action-oriented guy like Patrick would see in a city girl like her, but she found him completely fascinating. She loved the fact that nothing—absolutely nothing—fazed him. He didn't seem to know the meaning of the word *fear.*

Not that she would want to try half the things he had tried—definitely not hang gliding or parachuting from a plane—but she was terribly impressed that he had.

He was still looking at her, she noticed. In fact, he'd hardly taken his eyes off her all night. She felt that wash of heat again, and found herself thinking about how deliciously quiet and private their rooms were, tucked away from the lodge, next to the lake.

He reached for one of her hands. "I hope I'm not out of line in asking this, but...do you ever date your clients?"

She felt a rush of pleasure and an instinctive urge to say yes, then good sense kicked in. "No, I don't. At least— I never have." What sort of answer was that? She'd never dated a client because, until now, she'd never had one.

Suddenly she felt as if she was choking on all the lies she'd told in the past few days. What would Patrick say if she told him the truth now? He would understand... wouldn't he?

Was she crazy? Of course, he wouldn't. His stakes in this case couldn't be higher. He was searching for *his son.* He'd be angry and upset…and he'd probably insist they head back to New York immediately.

And wouldn't that be a shame? They were so close to Stephen, she could just sense it. Later, she would tell him everything.

"Not getting involved with clients sounds like a smart rule." Patrick caressed her fingers as he slowly let her hand slip away from his. "But, I've always been a fan of breaking rules."

His gaze traveled down her neck and she honestly felt as if he was touching her there. She wished he would. Heavens. If he could make her yearn for him with just a look, what would his caresses be like?

She lowered her gaze to her cutlery. "Maybe once this case is over. After we've found your son. Maybe then."

Provided he was still speaking to her, once she told him who she really was.

He smiled with grace and resignation. "So be it. I respect your integrity." He picked up the dessert menu. "What do you say to chocolate raspberry torte?"

It sounded good to Nadine. But not as good as that other thing he had offered.

AFTER DINNER, A LATE NIGHT drink in the lounge, then a game of pool in the second-floor games room, Patrick walked Nadine to her room, unlocking her door and handing her the key. He was determined to be a perfect gentleman, even though his desire for her had grown stronger with each passing minute of their evening together.

He had loved watching her eat. Her manners were absolutely impeccable, but she savored her food with such gusto. And she was a crackerjack with a pool cue. Another unexpected skill from a woman who was in the process of stealing his heart.

"Good night, Nadine. Are you okay with an early start tomorrow?"

"Definitely." She smiled at him, then unexpectedly leaned over to kiss his cheek.

Her skin was unbelievably soft and her scent reminded him of spring air in D.C. when the cherry trees were blooming. He caught her around the waist, wanting to prolong the moment of contact. Her breath was hot against his face. He could feel the lushness of her curves that began just at the point where his hand touched her body.

He had never known a woman like this. So feminine and sweet in nature and appearance, yet also determined and capable, honest and principled.

Though he'd sworn he wouldn't, he kissed her back. This time on her mouth.

She tasted as sweet as he'd expected and her lips were plump and warm as they parted and the kiss deepened.

He stepped inside the room, almost carrying her with him, then shut the door with his foot.

Only one small lamp burned on a table near the bed, and the glow reflected in Nadine's eyes as she stared up at him. He waited for her to say something. Yes. No. Anything. But she just gazed up at him, and he couldn't help himself.

He kissed her again.

This time he slipped her coat off her body. He found

her scarf and slowly unwrapped her shoulders, revealing the curves of her cleavage, the smooth length of her arms.

He kissed her again.

This time she worked his jacket off his body, then dipped her graceful hands under his sweater and up his back. He shivered with pleasure and sweet anticipation.

"I want to see your breasts," he told her. "The bare length of your legs. Every sweet inch of you."

She nodded, then raised her hands. With one sweeping motion, he removed her dress, then stood back to look. With her eyes on his, she unfastened her bra and let it fall. Then stepped out of her panties.

And she was perfect.

He laid her on the bed so he could kiss every part of her. Along the way he shucked his sweater. Then disposed of his jeans. He felt her hands exploring.

"You are solid muscle."

"I'm lucky it's too dark for you to see all the scars."

"I love your muscles and I'd love the scars, too."

She kissed him again, and he held her close. In his arms she felt so womanly, so precious. He wanted her, desperately, but even more than that, he wanted to please her.

He blocked his mind to worries about the snow, the avalanche, his imminent meeting with his son.

For the next few hours, all he wanted to think about was Nadine.

CHAPTER EIGHT

PATRICK WOKE WITH THE VIVID recollection that he'd spent the night in Nadine's room. He rolled from his back to his side and reached out with both arms.

Nothing.

He opened his eyes. Where was she? The empty space next to him was still warm.

As his senses slowly cleared, he became aware of sounds from the washroom. A minute later, Nadine emerged, fully dressed from her turtleneck—which was the exact same chocolate shade as her eyes—to her dark blue jeans.

She made the briefest of eye contact with him before dusting her hands together. "You'd better hurry and pack. Didn't you say you wanted to make an early start?"

Without waiting for his answer, she bent over her own suitcase, reminding him nicely of some of the pleasures from last night.

"Slow down a minute." He swung his legs to the floor and ran a hand over his head. Sure enough, his hair was standing on end and he knew he needed a shave.

Still, was a good-morning hug too much to ask?

"I can't slow down. We have a lot to accomplish today. First we'll need to find out if the highway has been cleared. If so, we should leave as soon as possible."

He watched as she stuffed a zippered bag into her suitcase, then changed her mind and transferred it to her briefcase.

Finally, he got it.

"You're sorry about what happened last night."

"Of course, I regret that it happened." She looked around, and not spotting anything else to shove into her luggage, started to pace. "I told you that I couldn't get involved with a client. And what did I do? I promptly spent the night with my client."

She stopped and clasped a hand to her head. Her eyes, he saw, were shimmering with tears.

"It's not like I blame *you*," she added. "I'm the one with the conflict. I'm the one who was supposed to set the boundaries. I don't know what's the matter with me."

She finished by kicking her bag, not hard, just a tiny vent to the frustration she was clearly feeling.

"Are you sure that's the real reason you're upset? Maybe you're upset because you didn't enjoy yourself. Maybe I didn't—"

"Oh, you did," she assured him. "Last night was wonderful in every way. I can't remember the last time I had so much fun. Which is probably why I let it happen. But it still isn't right."

"I hope I didn't give you the impression that my intentions are frivolous."

She shook her head. "No. But, please. Can we not talk about it? I know it's silly to pretend it never happened. But could we try?"

He was surprised at how much her suggestion hurt.

He hoped he hadn't pushed too hard last night. He didn't think he had. Too bad she looked so adorable, even when she was upset. She couldn't have any idea how much he still longed to hold her. And kiss her.

But on another level, he understood and respected her need to maintain her integrity. The least he could do now was honor her wishes.

Besides, he couldn't deny his own strong urge to start looking for his son.

He reached for his jeans and stepped into them quickly. Then he grabbed his sweater, socks and jacket. He checked the pocket and found his room key.

"Okay, Nadine. We'll do this your way. For now. I'll be ready to leave in fifteen minutes. If the highway is clear, we'll make Kicking Horse Ski Resort before noon."

AS SOON AS PATRICK LEFT her room, Nadine headed for the main lodge. Her emotions were in a terrible tangle, but she was determined to stick with plan A, which was to pretend nothing had happened last night.

Later, when she could afford the time, she would relive the evening, the glorious highs of being with Patrick, followed by the terrible guilt of realizing she'd screwed up once again.

Right now, though, she was Nadine Kimble, private investigator, following a hot lead, and hoping for the breakthrough that would justify all the risks she'd taken so far.

Even with the worries she had on her mind, Nadine was impressed with how pretty the resort looked in daylight. Everywhere she looked the snow was pure and untouched. The boughs of the evergreen trees were heavy with their crystal-white frosting. The chalets and main lodge had been designed to nestle into the landscape as if they had grown there naturally.

As for the lake, there was no way to tell how beautiful it might be in the summer. Right now it was frozen and covered with snow. A section had been cleared for ice skating. In the far distance she could make out several cross-country skiers enjoying the fresh air.

Nadine stomped the snow off her boots, then entered the main building. A young man named Tyler was behind the desk this morning, and when she inquired about the avalanche, he assured her that no one had been hurt, the snowplows had been through and the highway was open again.

"May I use your phone? I'd like to call ahead to the Kicking Horse Resort."

"By all means." He invited her to use the phone in a private alcove, then busied himself with other tasks.

Nadine took a deep breath, crossed her fingers and dialed the number she'd dug out from her files. When the phone was answered, she asked if she could book a private ski lesson, and her call was rerouted.

A cheerful-sounding woman with an Aussie accent answered. "G'day. How can I help you?"

"I was hoping I could take a private ski lesson today. We're about to leave Emerald Lake Lodge. We should be at the hill by eleven."

"Do you have your own equipment?"

"No. I'll need to rent."

"Not a problem. Why don't we set something up for twelve o'clock. It's a Monday, so the hill is nice and quiet. The perfect time for a lesson."

"Um…I was wondering if I could request a specific instructor?"

"Sure. Who would you like?"

"Stephen Stone."

"Stephen?" There was a pause. "He's one of our newest instructors. May I ask how you heard of him?"

Nadine felt like doing a happy dance. He was there. Finally something was going right. "I'm from New York, too. I know his fath—family."

"Okay. Stephen it will be. Rent your equipment, then come to our office in the main lodge. You can pay with cash or credit card and we have a release for you to sign, as well."

Nadine hung up the phone, then went to the lounge to see if she could snag take-out coffees and muffins for the road. Patrick arrived just as the food was delivered.

"Breakfast? Thank you." He accepted one of the coffees and a blueberry-bran muffin. "Are you ready to leave? We're checked out and our bags are loaded on the bus."

She'd found his son. She was so happy she didn't even need her morning coffee to smile. "Yup. I'm all set."

He eyed her suspiciously. "You're in a very good mood all of a sudden."

She almost told him about her phone call, then decided against it. Better to meet the young man, make sure she had the right person, and *then* tell Patrick the good news. Hopefully there would be no more mistakes.

HALF AN HOUR LATER, THEY DROVE into the avalanche zone where they'd been stopped the previous night.

Snowplows had scraped the highway clear, but the evidence of what had happened was all too evident. The avalanche had cleared a hundred-foot swath down the face of the mountain, leaving behind a rubble of fallen trees and trampled snow.

Nadine felt a lump in her throat, as Patrick quickly sped through, and she didn't feel completely safe again until the town of Golden came into view.

They had to drive through the town to reach the resort. Golden itself wasn't especially impressive and Nadine began to wonder if Kicking Horse Resort would live up to its reputation.

But when they finally approached the expansive development, she wasn't disappointed.

"This part of the country is full of hidden gems," Patrick said. "I grabbed a bunch of pamphlets from the lobby this morning. Do you know there are lots of heli- and cat-ski operations around here?"

"Chairlifts are exciting enough for me."

While Patrick checked them in at the lodge, Nadine bought herself a half-day ski pass. When she returned, Patrick handed her a key. "You're on the second floor," he said. "I'm on the third."

She wondered if he'd purposefully arranged for them to be so far apart, but he didn't elaborate.

"The mountain is calling," he told her, "but I'm going to lock myself in my room until I get my writing done."

"I'll give you a call if—if I have anything to report."

Nadine was almost light-headed with excitement as she changed into her ski clothes, rented equipment, then went to the Day Lodge to pay for her lesson and fill out the required paperwork. She was told to meet her instructor by the Pioneer Chair.

"He'll be wearing a jacket like mine and he'll be watching out for you," the lady with the Aussie accent told her. "Good luck and have fun! We had about six inches of powder yesterday, so conditions are fabulous."

As soon as Nadine stepped outside, the intensity of the sunlight hit her, and she had to pull on her goggles. Her skis were propped up on a rack near the door, and she settled them on the snow, then snapped her boots into the bindings. Using her poles to propel herself forward on the level surface, she followed the signs to the Pioneer Chair.

It didn't take her long to spot her instructor. Patrick's son was tall and thin, like him, but not yet with his father's developed upper body. His helmet covered his head and goggles obscured his eyes, but he had the freckled face of a redhead.

"Nadine?" he asked as she approached.

"Yes."

"Good to meet you. We've got a great day, let's make the most of it. Why don't we start with you showing me what you can do? Would you like to start with a beginner run?"

Despite the lure of a beautiful day and all the fresh powder, Nadine couldn't care less about skiing. She lifted her goggles and squinted at the boy.

"Actually, I didn't book your time because I wanted a lesson. I just wanted a chance to talk to you."

"What?" He stiffened, his friendly voice suddenly wary.

"I'm a private investigator from New York City. I was hired by your father to find you."

"What?" Pushing against his poles, he slid backward a few feet.

"I know this must come as a shock, but after your mother passed away—"

"Stop." The young man held out one of his hands. "Don't say any more. I think you have the wrong guy."

No. It wasn't possible. "You're Stephen Stone, right?"

The kid just stared at her. Or she assumed he was staring. His darn goggles blocked out more than just UV rays.

"I called the resort this morning and asked for a private lesson with you. Your father—"

"Would you cut it out with that, already? I'm telling you, I'm not the right guy. Stephen Stone, he started working here, but he didn't like it. He left last night. The girl at the desk didn't know that when you spoke to her. But she asked me to fill in for him."

Nadine could not believe this. "Are you sure?"

"I'm a friend of his. My name's Zach. So, yeah. I'm sure."

"Where did Stephen go?" Oh, please, not back to New York. She'd been so sure that today she would find Patrick's son for him.

"He had another job offer in Lake Louise. He decided to give that a try."

"When did he leave Kicking Horse?"

"Last night, after dinner."

"There was an avalanche around seven. The highway was closed."

"Well, maybe he left earlier than that, because I know he made it through. He called me last night to let me know that everything was cool."

Nadine couldn't believe it. She and Patrick might very well have crossed paths with Stephen last night at some point on the highway.

"So." Zach slid his skis back and forth. "You want to go ahead with your lesson now?"

"I don't think so. Thanks, Zach. I'm sorry I wasted your time."

Wearily, Nadine returned to the Day Lodge. The thought of backtracking to Lake Louise was almost more than she could bear. Another hour and a half drive, with no guarantee of results when they finally arrived. With her luck, Stephen would have changed his mind again, and moved on to God-knows-where.

More words of wisdom from Nathan and Lindsay came back to her then. "You've got to be so damned persistent in this job."

Boy, were they right. There was only one thing she felt glad about as she tromped back to return her equipment.

At least she hadn't raised Patrick's hopes by telling him she'd found his son.

CHAPTER NINE

NADINE OFFERED TO DRIVE to Lake Louise, so Patrick
could continue working on his book. He'd been startled
when she'd told him the change in plans, but once he'd
understood that the trail was now leading somewhere
new, he'd reacted quickly, packing up his notes and
computer and lugging their bags back to the car.

The money they'd spent on the hotel room, her ski
pass, lesson and rentals...all wasted. They were quickly
working their way through that five thousand dollar advance, and what did she have to show for it?

So far, exactly nothing.

"I'm sorry about this," she said, noticing him staring
vacantly out the window, his computer open but untouched on his lap.

"It's not your fault. You're just doing your job."

"But you haven't had much time to concentrate on
your writing."

"Finding Stephen is more important. If you're
thinking that I regret coming with you, don't. If I'd
stayed in New York, I wouldn't have been able to
write at all."

If he hadn't come on the trip, then last night wouldn't
have happened, either. Nadine wondered if he'd thought

of that. Then realized, no, of course he hadn't. His son was the only thing on his mind right now. And that was as it should be. Stephen was the important thing. She hoped they were nearing the end of their search.

And yet she was beginning to feel as though she was on a wild-goose chase. That they would arrive at Lake Louise only to discover that Stephen had taken off *again*.

How long could they keep following the young man? At what point would Patrick decide to call off the search and fly them back to the city?

But she *had* to be successful. If she failed in this, she would never forgive herself.

Suddenly Patrick began typing. He started tentatively, then the words came faster. He didn't even seem to notice when they drove past the site of the avalanche. With her stomach clenched, Nadine upped her speed as much as she dared, and gave a sigh of relief when they finally left the avalanche zone behind.

She would never again underestimate the power of snow.

Or the danger of lying.

She'd called them "fibs" in the beginning, but now she saw how she had deluded herself into making the worst decision of her life. Not just professionally, but personally, too.

She liked Patrick in a way she'd never liked any man before. He was dynamic, exciting…sexy. He could have been the *one*.

But once they got back to New York, she would never see him again. When he found out she'd taken on his case under false pretenses, he'd be furious. Especially if she failed to find his son.

If only she'd directed him to Nathan or Lindsay, as she should have done. Then she might have met him for the first time that night at the Rain forest Charity Gala. He would have spotted her in the crowd, walked over and introduced himself, and they would have fallen in love.

But even that daydream was too much to hope for, she suspected. He might have been attracted to her, but that would fade once he discovered who she was—who her family was.

She'd only known him a short while, but it was long enough to suspect that he had little use for families like hers. Families with inherited wealth, who wore designer clothing and attended charity balls, and wrote big checks rather than risk getting dirty hands.

The ironic thing was, she felt the same way. All her life she'd known she didn't fit into the world where she'd been born. She wanted to make a difference. To do valuable work and contribute in a positive way.

So far, she hadn't been too successful.

Please let Stephen Stone be at the Lake Louise ski hill. Please.

AFTER AN HOUR AND A HALF on the road, Nadine came to the signs for Lake Louise. The town and hotels were to her right, the ski hill to the left. Nadine took the overpass to the ski hill and, ignoring the large parking lots on the side of the road, drove straight to the unloading zone in front of the Day Lodge.

"Let me run in and ask some questions before we go to town and book a room for the night."

Patrick closed his laptop. "I'm coming with you."

She wanted to argue, but there seemed little point. If

the news was disappointing, at least this way she wouldn't have to be the one to tell him.

After a pit stop in the washrooms, they located the administrative offices. As soon as Nadine mentioned her name, the middle-aged woman at the desk—a woman named Shannon with curly blond hair— snapped her fingers.

"Did you say Nadine Kimble? I have a message for you." She snatched a pink slip from a pile. "Stephen Stone would like you to meet him today after the lifts close, around four-thirty in the upstairs lounge."

"YOU DID IT, NADINE. YOU FOUND him."

They'd returned to the car, neither one saying a word, as if they were afraid the bubble would burst.

Now Nadine fought an urge to wrap her arms around Patrick. He looked so happy and excited, and it tugged on her heart in the biggest way.

In that moment, she didn't care about proving her skills to Lindsay and the others. All she wanted was to see him reunited with the son he'd never known.

"We've got to do something to kill the next few hours. I know I'll never be able to write. How about we hit the slopes?"

She glanced at her watch. "By the time we rent equipment we'll be lucky to get an hour and a half on the slopes. It isn't worth it."

"What else are we going to do?"

There was a moment's silence as their eyes met. She could tell he was thinking about last night. About making love.

He put a hand on her waist and looked more deeply

into her eyes. "Two hours would pass all too quickly if we were in bed together."

She swallowed. Yes, they would. But she was supposed to have professional standards. And at this point she knew she wanted to be more than a diversion to keep him from thinking about meeting his son.

"Maybe the skiing is a good idea, after all."

THE RUNS AT LAKE LOUISE were gloriously long and Nadine was glad Patrick had talked her into trying them out. She didn't think his technique was any better than hers, but he was much stronger and totally fearless, flying off ledges and taking jumps that she was too cautious to try.

At three-thirty they were on the quad chair, going up for their last run. The hill was very quiet and they had the chair to themselves. Aside from the humming of the motorized lift, the silence was absolute.

On their other rides up the mountain, Patrick had been talkative, sharing his excitement at the conditions and comparing the terrain here to other places he had seen.

Now, though, he seemed lost in thought, and she didn't need to wonder what about.

"Would you prefer to meet Stephen on your own?" she asked.

The suggestion seemed to surprise him. Then he considered it. "Maybe after a while you could leave us to get acquainted. If Stephen seems willing. I'm still expecting a lot of anger."

"His friend Zach must have called him and told him we were on our way. At least he's had a few hours to get used to the idea that he's about to meet his father."

She'd kind of ambushed Zach at Kicking Horse earlier today, Nadine realized. In some respects she was glad that he hadn't turned out to be Stephen after all.

"I keep trying to put myself in his shoes," Patrick said. "I'm hoping he'll be more curious than upset, but you never know. Especially when he's only recently lost his mother. He's still got to be pretty shaken up by that."

And here they were, dropping another emotional bombshell on the boy. But it couldn't be helped. It was his mother, after all, who had set up the chain of events. Patrick was only reacting as any responsible man would do.

The light was already getting flat as they made their last run of the day, making it difficult to read the terrain. Nadine followed Patrick cautiously as he skied right up to the rental shop, where they returned their equipment and retrieved their regular footwear.

A few dozen people were already sitting at the tables by the windows when they walked into the lounge at exactly four-thirty. Nadine was scrutinizing their faces when Patrick grasped her arm.

"That must be him."

He nodded toward the vacant tables at the back of the lounge. There, almost hidden in the shadows was a solitary young man. His helmet, with goggles attached, was on the table next to a glass of beer.

He looked approachable, but nervous. As for his hair, it was red, all right. He'd exaggerated the color with some sort of dye and had ended up with a shade that was almost magenta.

"What has he done with his hair?" Patrick muttered.

"At least he doesn't have a lot of facial piercings," she said to console him. "The hair will grow out."

They moved forward together. Nadine knew this would be a moment that Patrick would remember for the rest of his life. She thought regretfully about her camera, which was stowed in the trunk of her rental car.

But there were a few bridges to cross before it would be appropriate to start snapping photos.

This was her job, she remembered. She'd better step forward and make introductions.

She approached the boy first, drawing his gaze from Patrick. "Stephen Stone?"

He stood, smiled slightly, then the nervous look returned. "Hi. You're the private investigator?"

"I am. Nadine Kimble. And this is Patrick O'Neil. Your mother had a letter mailed to him about six weeks ago. He was in Alaska and didn't read it until last week. But he came as soon as we could find you."

She didn't need to say more. Zach would have told him that she'd been hired by his father. She watched as the two men shook hands cautiously.

"Sit down," Patrick said. "I want to tell you the whole story—or at least as much as I know about the story. And I want to give you a letter your mother wrote for *you*."

PATRICK PULLED THE ENVELOPE out of a zippered pocket in his jacket. Before leaving New York, he'd placed it in a plastic bag for protection. He slid it across the table to Stephen.

How surreal this is, he thought. The setting—a lounge on a ski hill—hardly seemed an appropriate place for a boy to meet his father for the first time in his life.

Though, given the love of skiing that they shared, maybe it was as fitting a place as possible.

Stephen still looked nervous. He touched the plastic bag but made no effort to remove the envelope.

"You say m-my mother wrote this?"

"It was included with the letter that she wrote to me. You see, Stephen, until I read that letter I had no idea that your mother was pregnant when we broke up. I had absolutely no idea you even existed."

"No idea? None at all? How is that possible? You did get M-Mom pregnant, right?"

"We used birth control. Obviously not as carefully as we should have. But it never occurred to me that it hadn't been effective." Hell, that hadn't come out right. He didn't want to make the boy feel like his existence was just a mistake.

He glanced helplessly at Nadine, hoping she would help untangle his words for him.

She gave him a sympathetic look. "As soon as your father knew about you, he tried to find you. Unfortunately it wasn't easy. He ended up hiring our firm and we were able to trace you, through your aunt Diane, to Calgary. From there it's been a guessing game as we've traveled from one ski resort to another."

"It seemed we were always one step behind you," Patrick added. With hindsight, he could see the humor in the situation, though at the time the tension had almost killed him.

Stephen asked a few more questions. Was he married? Did he have other kids?

Patrick answered the boy honestly, but when he tried to ask questions in return, Stephen was evasive—especially when they had to do with his mother.

"I can't talk about her yet."

Patrick understood. He remembered the pain of losing his own mother. The first six months were the worst. After that, a sense of emptiness had stayed with him for a long time.

Nadine cleared her throat. "I think I'll check out the gift shop. Stephen, it was very nice to meet you. Take your time here," she added to Patrick, before she left.

Patrick was quiet for a moment. He couldn't believe the boy sitting across from him was really his son. He realized he'd expected to feel some sort of immediate connection with the boy. But he didn't.

Maybe it would come in time. If Stephen was willing to let him be part of his life.

"I know this is weird," he said. "But I'd like the chance to get to know you. If you ever want to come back to New York, I'll buy you a plane ticket. I've got tons of air miles."

"What do you do?" Stephen asked. "I mean, for a living? Are you some kind of businessman?"

"Actually I'm a travel writer. When I get home, I'll mail you some of my books." He waited for some sign that Stephen was impressed, or at least interested, but the boy remained stoic.

Patrick swallowed. The emotion of this meeting was getting to him, and his voice was growing hoarse. "Another thing. If you decide you want to go on to college next fall, I'd be glad to help you out."

Diane had told Nadine that Stephen was registered at a college near Boston. He waited for Stephen to mention it, but he didn't.

All he did was sigh. "Look. You've given me a lot to process. I need time to think."

"Of course." Patrick handed him a business card. "You can phone or e-mail anytime."

Stephen nodded, then stood. He grabbed his helmet and shifted awkwardly. "So. I guess I'll be seeing you."

Patrick nodded. Then he noticed the letter from June, still encased in the plastic bag. "Hang on. You almost forgot this."

He passed Stephen the letter and watched as he stuffed it into his jacket pocket.

He couldn't help feeling disappointed. He'd hoped Stephen would read the letter in front of him and tell him what June had written. More than anything, he longed for a fuller explanation of why June had kept this secret for so long.

But he couldn't blame Stephen for wanting to read the letter in private. After all, to him, Patrick was just a stranger.

CHAPTER TEN

NADINE'S ADRENALINE WAS STILL surging fifteen minutes after she'd left Patrick alone with his son. Too restless to sit, she prowled through the gift shop, finally purchasing bottled Canadian maple syrup and a sweatshirt for Martha. Her parents had no interest in touristy gifts, but their housekeeper would appreciate the thought and Nadine knew she'd make excellent use of the syrup.

Since Patrick still hadn't appeared, she ordered a hot chocolate then stood by the entrance to wait for him.

She was hugely relieved that she had pulled it off. She'd found Stephen and Patrick was finally getting to talk to his son. Their first meeting was going okay—not fabulous, but not terrible, either. Stephen seemed more confused than angry.

Though maybe anger would come later.

It was hard to imagine what it must be like for him. To have gone through his life thinking his father was dead. And then to have him show up out of the blue.

In some ways it would seem like a dream come true, she supposed. But he must also feel cheated, for all the years he'd lost.

She finished her drink and had just tossed the cup in the trash when Patrick's son came racing down the stairs.

She called out his name, but Stephen didn't even seem to notice her. He was pulling out his cell phone as he ran out the door—probably calling Zach to let him know how the meeting had gone.

A few minutes later, Patrick came down the stairs, moving a lot more slowly than Stephen had, his face showing signs of the emotional toll the meeting had taken. She waited until he was near then asked, "You okay?"

If she wasn't self-conscious after their night together, she would have given him a hug. As it was, she just touched his arm in a supportive gesture.

He reacted with a weak, brief smile. "I think so."

He was clearly overwhelmed. "We'd better get a room in Lake Louise for the night," she said. At some point they'd need to book flights home. But right now Patrick had enough on his mind.

They made their way outside. Nadine took a long look at the mountain panorama, and a deep breath of the clear air. It seemed unbelievable that tomorrow at this time she'd be back in the heart of New York City. Some day, she promised herself, she would come back here for a real ski holiday.

Then she climbed into the driver side of the Subaru. She didn't even ask if Patrick wanted to drive—he was clearly exhausted.

She stopped at a hotel close to the highway that looked reasonably comfortable, and Patrick went through the process of booking them two rooms again.

Nadine was tired by now, too, but there was something she needed to talk to Patrick about before they left this place.

"Want to grab something for dinner?" she asked.

"I'm not hungry, but you must be starved. We didn't have lunch, did we?"

She was hungry, but right now that wasn't topping her list of priorities. She just wanted a few quiet moments alone with Patrick.

They were seated in a dining room that obviously catered to families. A mother and a father and their three little boys were noisily and happily enjoying their meal at the table closest to them. An elderly couple, with windblown faces and dressed in ski gear, sat at the next table over, smiling indulgently at the family.

Friendly people, Nadine thought, though for what she planned to say, a little more privacy would have been nice. She slid her hands over the polyester tablecloth, then glanced at the laminated menu.

"It's not the Emerald Lake Lodge, is it?" Patrick asked.

"No, but it will do." There would never be another night like the one they'd spent at that remote mountain paradise. Nadine thought it was probably best that this place was turning out to be so different.

They both ordered steak and salad and a glass of red wine. With the ordering out of the way, Patrick seemed to lose the last of his energy. He sagged into his chair and sighed.

"How are you feeling?"

"I don't know. Tired, mostly." His eyes lit up a bit as he looked at her. "Thank you. I haven't said it yet, but I mean it with all my heart. Thank you for finding him for me. And thank you for being there when I met him."

"Y-you're welcome." She should tell him the truth now, Nadine thought. She should tell him she was just a receptionist who had decided she was ready for more responsibility. She'd proved that she was capable, right? After all, she'd found his son. How upset could he be that she hadn't been honest with him from the start?

But deep inside, she knew that he *would* be upset.

And how much truth should she tell him? Should she also mention that her last name was Waverly and that her family owned the hotel chain of the same name and, yes, she was related to the blonde actress/model/attention-seeker, Liz Waverly, who was always on the cover of one entertainment magazine or another.

She could just imagine how Patrick would react to all *that*.

Maybe she owed him the truth. Her conscience was nagging her to come clean. But not today. Not after all he'd been through.

"I just thought of something. Now that you've found Stephen, I'm not your client anymore," he said.

"Until we're back in the city, yes, you are," she insisted.

"Pity. Does that mean you're not up for a game of pool? They have a table in the games room, I'm told."

"That's big talk from someone who can hardly keep his eyes open."

He laughed. "Yeah. I guess an early night would be a good idea. You know, it's the damnedest thing. I was so worked up about meeting Stephen, and now that it's happened—well, I feel kind of letdown. Deep inside I was hoping there would be more of a connection between us. But he just seemed like another kid to me. Isn't that terrible?"

Nadine was enough of a romantic to agree. But she wasn't about to tell him so. She wanted him to feel better, not worse. "It's going to take time for both of you to adjust."

"I suppose…"

"But that does bring me to a very important subject. Patrick, I think you and Stephen should have your DNA tested."

Immediately he stiffened. "We already talked about this. You know how I feel."

"It's a very simple test. I've brought a kit with me. We just need a sample of your saliva and his. The results will be back in a few days and the lab we use guarantees almost one hundred percent accuracy."

"I appreciate the advice, but if June says he's my kid, then he's my kid. Today was awkward enough as it was. I'm not going to ask Stephen for a sample of his DNA."

THE NEXT DAY, PATRICK DROVE the Subaru back to the Calgary airport. When he'd booked the flight the night before, there had been only two economy seats available for the Calgary-Toronto leg of the trip. Nadine insisted he take the spot by the window so he could work on his book, leaving her wedged between him and a businessman from Los Angeles.

Patrick wrote furiously for most of the flight. Finding Stephen had taken an enormous load off his conscience and now his pressing book deadline was at the top of his priority list.

That didn't stop him from being very aware of the woman by his side. Her perfume, the way she tucked her hair behind her ears when she read, her addiction to lip gloss, which she put on every hour or so—these small things were constantly drawing his gaze to her.

Patrick had spent a lot of time traveling and he'd learned that you could tell a great deal about a person from the way they treated flight attendants, taxi drivers, the stranger sitting next to them on the plane.

Nadine was unfailingly polite. More than that, she was kind, and her sweetness, in turn, seemed to bring out the best in the people she met.

With Nadine, problems were smoothed over, uncomfortable situations drew a laugh and complaining was never an option.

He admired her style.

Every now and then he thought of Stephen. He wondered if June's son would take up his offer and fly to New York for a visit. He hoped that Stephen would. He knew during their two hours together, they'd barely scratched the surface of what they had to learn about each other.

An idea for a father-son skiing trip began to take shape in his mind…then he realized they were hardly at that stage, yet. Maybe they never would be. Wearily, he turned his attention back to his writing.

They landed in New York before midnight on Tuesday. As Patrick hauled their suitcases into the back of a taxi, he reflected that so much had happened, he felt like a different man than the one who had packed this suitcase four short days ago.

On the drive to Manhattan, Nadine was quiet. He wondered if she was glad that their time together was ending.

Or did she, like him, hope that their time together was actually beginning?

He touched her shoulder. She'd been looking out her

window for so long, he was beginning to think she was avoiding him. "Will you have dinner with me on Saturday night?"

She shifted uneasily. "Won't you be busy with your writing?"

"I allow myself breaks for meals."

She sighed. "I still don't think it's a good idea."

"If you're worried about my deadline—"

"No. Patrick, a lot has happened on this trip."

Wasn't that the truth.

"You need some time to let it all sink in. And I need some time to process, too."

"But I thought, once I wasn't your client—"

"The dust hasn't fully settled on that, either. Let me write my final report and send you an invoice."

"And then…?"

"We'll see."

There was much she wasn't saying. He had no idea what was troubling her, or how to get her to open up to him again, the way she had that night at the Emerald Lake Lodge.

Maybe she was just tired. He hoped that was it.

As they drove over the bridge into Manhattan, the driver asked, "Where to now?"

Nadine gave him Patrick's address.

He frowned. "I'd rather you were dropped off first."

"Your place is closer," she countered.

He couldn't argue with that because he had no idea where she lived.

He was suddenly struck by how much she knew about him, and how little he knew about her. Was that because she was naturally a better listener than a talker?

Or had she purposefully guarded her privacy? Maybe he'd mistaken her natural warmth and kindness for something more.

Maybe he wasn't even the first client she'd spent the night with.

No. He couldn't believe that she hadn't shared at least some of his feelings. She hadn't just been passionate and giving with her lovemaking, but also warm and affectionate in the hours after.

With her in his arms, he'd known he was holding something rare and precious. Now, as she sat quietly beside him, so close, but in reality very far away, he could feel what they'd had—what he'd thought they had—slipping through his fingers.

NORMALLY NADINE HAD NO TROUBLE falling asleep but that night she got a taste of what life was like for chronic insomniacs like Lindsay. She longed for the respite of sleep, but her mind kept flashing back to special moments she'd spent with Patrick. The way he'd laughed, both impressed and disbelieving, when she'd beat him at pool. His amazing grace and speed on the ski hill. His habit of smiling at her during odd moments when she was doing something utterly routine, like reapplying her lip gloss.

Then there were the memories of making love, and these were the most distracting of all. She'd never had a man kiss her or touch her quite the way that Patrick had. He'd made her feel utterly desirable and precious.

Nadine tossed restlessly in bed. She'd wanted to say yes when he'd asked her out to dinner. But she couldn't accept another date with him until he knew the whole truth about her. She was paying the price for her deception now. If she had been honest from the beginning, Patrick would probably be in bed with her tonight. Now—he might never be again.

When the light of dawn finally inched through the slats of her blinds, she would have been grateful except for one thing. She had to go to work. And going to work meant telling the others what she had done.

In her daydreams this was supposed to be her moment of triumph. She'd solved her first case. Lindsay, Nathan and Kate, awed at her skill and resourcefulness, immediately invited her to be a partner. She was given her own office, and new business cards that read Nadine Kimble, Private Investigator.

But now—one and a half hours later—as she unlocked the door to the office, she felt only shame and remorse.

There was only so often you could fib, bend the truth and lie by omission before you started to feel your integrity being stripped away. Proving she could handle the job had not been worth the price she'd paid.

Nadine started a fresh pot of coffee, anxious for someone to show up so she could make her confession and get it over with. But when Lindsay and Nathan finally arrived, at ten minutes to nine, they clearly had their minds on other matters.

"Thank God, you're back." Lindsay handed Nathan her coat, then brushed her windswept hair off her face. "This place has been crazy without you. I have a new client coming in ten minutes, and after that I have appointments outside the office for the rest of the day."

"Did you have a good holiday?" Nathan asked, hanging his and Lindsay's coats in the closet.

Before Nadine could answer, he added, "If you're not

too busy, I could use some help with background checks. I've got a batch that's due at the end of the week and I'm running late because I've been handling Kate's work, too."

"Why have you—"

"That's the other thing," Lindsay said. "Kate's OB has put her on bed rest. Can you believe it?"

"Is she okay? And the baby?"

"Physically they're both fine, but mentally…well you can imagine how much Kate loves bed rest."

"Poor Jay."

"Yes, exactly." At the sound of approaching footsteps from the hall, Lindsay groaned. "Just my luck. My client must be early. Nadine, can you bring us coffee in the boardroom?" She paused long enough to kiss Nathan, then disappeared into her office.

As a worried-looking, middle-aged woman stepped into reception, Nadine resigned herself to the fact that her confession was going to have to wait awhile.

IT WASN'T UNTIL AFTER TEN that the office finally grew quiet enough for Nadine to start on the paperwork for Patrick's case. Lindsay and Nathan were gone for the day and the phone had stopped ringing. Nadine started with the billing, calculating her hours and applying the total against the advance Patrick had given her.

It turned out that he owed her several hundred dollars, but as he had picked up all the travel expenses of their trip, she decided not to bill him. She printed a copy of the invoice, attached Patrick's check to it, then left it in Nathan's in-tray to be included in his next batch of deposits.

Next she worked on her official case report. She'd

written these countless times for the others, transcribing tapes and notes into the proper format:

The following investigation was conducted by Nadine Kimble, of The Fox & Fisher Detective Agency, in New York City. On November 2, Patrick O'Neil asked for help in locating his biological son…

For several hours she labored over the report. The mistake she'd made in not obtaining a photo of Stephen still rankled, and she decided that, better late than never, she should find one for the file.

She decided to write his aunt Diane and ask for one. She included a postage-paid envelope and also her e-mail address so Diane could send a digital photo if that was easier.

At two o'clock Nadine paused to eat a dry bagel with cream cheese and helped herself to one of the juice smoothies that Kate loved. She made a mental note to visit Kate tomorrow morning and see if there was anything she could do for her.

Her snack finished, Nadine returned to the report. It was more difficult to write than she'd expected. She kept including details that didn't belong, kept having to backspace over information about Patrick and his life and the things they'd done together that had nothing to do with finding Stephen.

Like skiing, and playing pool, and having a candlelight dinner and making love…

No, it wouldn't do at all to include *those* details in her report.

When she was finally finished, she printed a copy for the files and a copy for Patrick.

Then, she realized that this report said everything that needed to be said to the partners. This report, in short, could be her confession.

She printed off three more copies of the report, stapling them into five neat packages—for Patrick, the files, Lindsay, Nathan and Kate. As she worked, she reflected that she might be taking the coward's way out, but at least she could go to sleep tonight with a clear conscience.

CHAPTER ELEVEN

PATRICK TRIED TO WRITE ALL DAY Wednesday but his attention span was frustratingly short. Every time his phone rang he expected to hear Stephen's voice on the line. Or Nadine's.

But it was never them.

Nadine had said she would get in touch after she'd finished her final report. He wondered how long it would take. He wanted to talk to her. Wanted to see her and touch her.

Ask her opinion on what he should do about his son.

He was beginning to think he'd made a mistake leaving it up to Stephen to make the next move. What if the boy never wanted to see him again? Maybe there had been something in June's letter that painted him as the bad guy.

Damn, he wished he'd read that letter when he had the chance. He could have resealed it in a new envelope and Stephen wouldn't have been the wiser.

Patrick pressed his fist against his forehead. He felt like he was going mad. If only June had told him about this face-to-face. He had so much he wanted to ask her, but she'd planned this whole thing so he couldn't.

She must have known how crazy this would make him.

But to be fair, she'd had bigger problems on her mind.

Patrick tried again to focus on his manuscript. For a short while he was able to concentrate, but before he knew it, he was staring out the window and thinking about Nadine again.

She'd asked him to wait until he received her final invoice and report in the mail before contacting her again. And he intended to respect that. The key word being *intended*.

Early Thursday morning, after a very long night with very little sleep, he went out for a walk. Forty-five minutes later, he stopped in front of The Fox & Fisher Detective Agency and told himself that this self-enforced exile was silly. Why couldn't they at least have a coffee together…was that too much to ask?

Posted office hours were nine to five and it was only quarter to nine now. Deciding to take a chance Nadine might be in early, he went inside, through the vestibule and up the stairs to the second floor.

THURSDAY MORNING, NADINE decided to stop by Kate and Jay's new apartment before she went to the office. Last night, she'd bought a case of smoothies and some magazines she thought Kate might enjoy.

Nadine took her report on Patrick O'Neil's case and slipped it between the pages of one of the magazines. She was too much of a coward to hand the report directly to Kate.

At the front door of the apartment building, Nadine ran into Jay and his teenage nephew, Eric. Jay was a tall, distinguished man—the sort of guy strangers would automatically turn to in an emergency.

He also had the softest heart.

After his sister's death, when Eric had first come to live with him, he'd sidelined his career so he could spend time with his grief-stricken nephew. For a few months he'd worked at Fox & Fisher, and during that time Nadine had become very fond of him.

She thought Kate—who longed for a big family—had found the perfect man to share in her dream.

"Hey, Nadine. Isn't it a workday?" Jay looked pleased to see her, but curious.

"Yes, I'm on my way to the office. I just wanted to drop off a few goodies for Kate first." She smiled at Eric. "How's school?"

"Good."

As he hitched his backpack over his shoulders, Nadine thought he'd probably grown two inches since she'd seen him last. He was fifteen now. A serious kid who dreamed of working for the NYPD one day.

"I'm off for the next three days," Jay said. "But I have a few errands, so I thought I'd walk to the subway with Eric. Go on up. Kate's going to be thrilled to have some female companionship for a change."

"Gotta get going, Uncle Jay. We have an exam first period and I can't be late."

Jay shrugged good-naturedly at his nephew's prodding. "Okay, let's make tracks. Catch you later, Nadine. It's the second door on the left."

This was Nadine's first visit to the three-bedroom apartment Kate and Jay had moved to after they were married. She knocked on the door, then tried the handle, glad to see it wasn't locked.

"It's just me. Nadine. Don't get up." She entered the

small foyer. To her right was the kitchen, with painted cabinets, tiled floors and bistro seating. To the left, a living room, where Kate was supine on an aqua-colored leather sofa.

"Hey, you! This is a nice surprise." Kate tossed the *New York Times* to the floor. "Did you bring presents?"

Nadine laughed as she scanned the warm, inviting room. "Wow, you've really fixed up the place." Lindsay had described it in less than flattering terms when they'd first moved in.

"It's home. Now show me the presents."

Nadine passed her the stack of magazines, with her report tucked deeply in the middle. She'd hidden it well, since she didn't want to be here when Kate read it. Then she opened the grocery bag. "I brought those smoothies you like. I'll put them in the fridge."

"Thanks, Nadine. You're a sweetheart. This is so boooring, you wouldn't believe it. And I'm only on my second day!"

Nadine returned from the kitchen and sat on the chair next to the sofa. "Why did your OB put you on bed rest?"

"She's worried about premature birth. My due date is only three weeks away, but she said the baby was small and she wants to delay labor for at least another week. So basically, I'm supposed to keep my activity to a minimum and my eating to a maximum."

Nadine laughed. "That doesn't sound too bad. But what about the wedding? Are you going to be able to go?"

"I'll be bringing the baby with me, but I wouldn't miss it. Even if Jay has to push me in a wheelchair. Now tell me about your holiday. Lindsay said you ducked away for a few days. So is he cute?"

Nadine lost her smile.

"Oh, no. What went wrong?"

"It's complicated. I can't talk about it now. Tomorrow I'll visit again. Maybe by then…" By then Kate would have read the case summary and she would have talked to Lindsay and Nathan.

Who knew—by then she may have been fired.

Nadine asked if there was anything she could do, and after Kate assured her, "Jay will be home in an hour anyway, and he loves being my personal slave," there was no more putting it off.

Nadine headed for the office.

THE FOX & FISHER DETECTIVE Agency appeared to be open when Patrick tried the door, though the reception desk was vacant. Beyond reception were two offices. Both had their doors partway open providing a glimpse of a man and a woman, both preoccupied with work.

Patrick decided to wait until one of them noticed him.

Eventually a man emerged from the office on the left. He looked like a cop to Patrick. He had an honest, clean-scrubbed face combined with the sort of physique you didn't want to meet up with in a back alley.

"Sorry. Our receptionist seems to be late. I'm Nathan Fisher. Do you have an appointment?" He paused, narrowed his eyes. "Wait a minute. Aren't you that guy who writes adventure travel books?" He snapped his fingers. "Patrick O'Neil."

"That's me." He held out his hand and smiled. It was always nice being recognized. Maybe because it didn't happen that often. "And, no, I'm afraid I don't have an appointment but I'm here to see—"

"Holy crap!"

The expletive came from the office next to Nathan's. A blonde woman with delicate coloring and a lean, athletic build, emerged from her office, wearing a blazer, top, jeans…and socks. She had papers in her hand.

"Did you read this report from Nadine?" She looked up, surprised to see a third person in the room. "I'm sorry. I thought we were alone in here." She glanced at the receptionist's desk. "Damn. She still isn't in?"

"Not yet," Nathan Fisher said calmly. "I haven't read the report, but we can talk about it later. This is Patrick O'Neil. He wrote that travel book on New Zealand that we were looking at last night."

The conversation had been confusing enough, but now Patrick was genuinely puzzled. "My New Zealand book? But—" Before he could say that it wouldn't be on the shelves for a couple more weeks, he remembered that he hadn't seen his copy since his first meeting with Nadine last week. He must have left it behind.

"It's a terrific book." Nathan went on enthusing. "Lindsay and I are thinking of traveling there for our honeymoon."

"The two of you are getting married. Congratulations."

"Fox," Lindsay said, pointing to herself, "and Fisher," she concluded, indicating her fiancé. "But I know who you are. You're the fellow who was looking for his son."

"He is?" Nathan asked.

"Yes." Patrick said at the same time.

Nathan rubbed his head. "Am I missing something here?"

Patrick was having the same feeling. "I was actually

hoping to speak with one of your colleagues. Nadine Kimble. Is she in the office?"

Nathan gave him a puzzled look. "Nadine is our—"

"Out for the morning," Lindsay interrupted, loudly, and rather rudely, Patrick thought. "She's out for the morning and I don't know—"

Lindsay stopped short as the outer door started to open, and a woman entered the office. Even before he saw her face, Patrick knew it was Nadine. She was barely in the room and he could already smell her perfume.

"Oh," she said, stopping short at the door. She stared at him, clearly surprised—and not in a happy way— to see him.

At just that moment, Patrick noticed a nameplate on the receptionist's desk. Why was Nadine's nameplate on the receptionist's desk?

He flashed back to his first time in this office. Nadine had been sitting at that desk. She'd said the receptionist was out of the office.

But why would she have lied? Why would she have pretended…? He shook his head. No. That wasn't Nadine. There had to be an explanation.

"Nadine?" he asked. "What the hell is going on here?"

Nadine looked beyond him to the people she worked with. Nathan Fisher looked almost as confused as Patrick felt right now.

His partner, Lindsay Fox, seemed to have a handle on the situation, though.

"I just read your report, Nadine," she said. "We'll have to talk later. But for now, why don't you take your—client—into the boardroom so you can straighten things out with him?"

Looking guilt-stricken, Nadine nodded. Then she turned back to Patrick. "May I pour you some coffee?"

The blurred picture was coming into focus now. And he didn't care about coffee. "I'd rather you told me what's going on. Why is your name on the receptionist's desk?"

She sighed deeply. "You noticed that, huh?"

"Just a second ago." He had a vague remembrance of her shifting files around on that first day and now he understood why. She'd been hiding the sign. She'd purposefully deceived him.

"Let me explain. Let's go in the conference room. Please?"

The others had retreated to their offices, but rather than discuss this in the open, he agreed. She led him into the room where they'd discussed his case the first time, and closed the door. As soon as they were alone, she apologized.

"I'm sorry. I was going to tell you."

"So it's true? You're just a receptionist?" He couldn't believe he'd been duped so thoroughly.

She cringed. "Not *just* a receptionist. I've taken classes and I've worked on plenty of cases with the others. It's just—yours was the first case I've handled on my own."

"So I was your guinea pig?" And she really thought that would make him feel better?

"I found your son, didn't I?"

"That's not the point. I came here thinking I was hiring an experienced private investigator. You can't pretend you didn't sign me on under false pretenses."

She'd been standing behind one of the chairs, as if needing a barrier between them. Now she gripped the back of the chair. "I don't know why I'm arguing. Of course, you're right. I was dishonest from the start. I thought as long as I was successful, it wouldn't matter."

"The end justifies the means? I can't believe you would even say that." How had he been so wrong about her? "You turned finding my son into some sort of game."

"That's not fair. I worked hard."

"And working hard excuses you from lying?"

She dropped her gaze. "No."

"Well, you were damned good at it. You not only convinced me you were a private investigator, you also had me half falling in love with you." He laughed bitterly. What a bloody, blind fool he'd been.

"Patrick, please believe me when I say how sorry I am. I—I felt those same feelings…for you."

"I have to give it to you. You know how to make a pretty apology. What's the matter? Are you worried I'll make a stink with your employer? Maybe lodge a complaint against the agency?"

He could do that. He had every right. In fact, maybe he should try to make some trouble for her.

"No. That isn't what I was worried about," she said quietly, but firmly.

Seeing tears pooling in her eyes, he had to look away from her. Damn it, she was still getting to him. He swallowed and clenched his teeth. *Don't be an idiot. Why should I feel sorry for her? This is probably just another great acting job on her part.*

"Whatever you feel—I don't care," he said. He was trying to stay focused on his anger, but the pain of being deceived was even stronger. He had to get out of here. "Go ahead and send me your report and the invoice. I'll pay it. Like you said, you did deliver the results."

As he turned to leave, she said, "Stop. Wait. There's one more thing I need to tell you."

Slowly every muscle in his body turned to stone. *One more thing?* Good God, what could it be?

She moved so she could see his face and he reluctantly met her resolute gaze. She must have wiped away her tears because they were gone and there were dark smudges under her eyes.

"I want you to know my real name."

He felt stunned. "You're not Nadine Kimble? But the sign on your desk—"

"Kimble is my mother's maiden name. I use it at work. My legal name is Nadine Kimble Waverly."

His mind remained blank for a moment. Then he remembered seeing her at the gala, how at home she had appeared in the diamond ballroom of the…*Waverly* Hotel. "Your parents are Wilfred and Sophia?"

She nodded.

He covered his eyes with his hands. The Waverlys were beyond rich, beyond wealthy. She might as well have told him she was a Trump or a Kennedy, the name had that much weight.

He looked at her again, this time focusing on the expensive-looking clothes, the Patek Philippe watch. "What the hell are you even doing here?"

"I—I wanted a real job."

"I'll bet. Great concept for a reality TV show. Rich socialite becomes private investigator… Isn't that the sort of thing your cousin is famous for?"

Because, of course, Nadine must be related to that blonde flake he'd seen on magazine covers and, briefly, on the TV before he could change the channel. What was her name…Liz, that was it. Patrick couldn't believe how quickly the puzzle pieces were falling into place.

Or what an ugly picture was forming.

PATRICK DIDN'T SAY A WORD of farewell. Perhaps he thought his parting look of disgust said it all. Nadine sank into the chair she'd been leaning on and started to cry.

She knew she'd been in the wrong.

But had she deserved all his contempt and scorn?

Perhaps she had. He'd hired her to find his son, a job that was intensely important and personal to him. And she had not been the person she'd made herself out to be.

No matter what, she was not going to shrivel up and run away. One piece of advice her father often repeated suddenly came to mind. *When you make a mistake— face it head-on.*

Nadine went to the box of tissues they kept on hand for distressed clients and took a handful. Using the reflection off the glass covering one of the paper clip pictures, she cleaned up her face.

She straightened her shoulders.

Then went out to deal with Lindsay and Nathan.

They were hanging out in Lindsay's office, each holding a copy of her report. The looks they gave her as she approached were beyond incredulous.

Nathan offered her his chair, but she kept standing.

"I—I suppose you're going to ask for my r-resignation?"

Or were they going to fire her? She'd never get another real job if they did that. She'd have to go back to her parents and ask to work at the foundation.

It would be worthwhile work, she knew. But—

"No." Lindsay sounded surprised she would even suggest it. "You're an important part of the team. You think we're going to dump you because of one mistake?"

"A rather significant mistake," Nathan added. "Bordering on fraudulent."

"Still, it took balls to do what you did."

Nadine couldn't believe it. Lindsay seemed *impressed*. Nathan, less so, but then Nathan was a by-the-rules kind of guy.

"I see this as partly our fault," Nathan said. "You kept asking for more responsibility, you *earned* the right to more responsibility, and we kept putting you off."

"But—I lied to one of our clients. And...I kind of did the same thing to both of you. And to Kate."

"Like I said, it was a mistake," Lindsay agreed. She lifted the report in the air. "But you provided good service to the client. You gave him exactly what he wanted."

If only they knew, Nadine thought, feeling her cheeks grow hot. "Looking back, I think I could have saved time if I'd done a few things differently."

"That's the nature of the business," Nathan said. "You think Lindsay and I don't feel that way at the end of almost every case? We all handle situations differently. We all learn to be more efficient as we gain experience."

"That's one of the reasons you should be working with a partner for your first year as an active investigator," Lindsay said.

Nadine wondered if she could possibly be hearing correctly. "Are you saying I'm not fired?"

"Like we can afford to fire you," Lindsay said bluntly. "We're already losing Kate."

"We've been talking," Nathan continued. "Once we've

hired a new receptionist, we'll shift you to full-time investigative work. You'll start out working with me."

"Then after he's taught you how to do things the correct way, you'll come and learn a few bad habits from me." Finally Lindsay cracked a smile.

Nadine almost laughed with relief. "You're serious? I'm going to be a full-time P.I.?"

"Damn right," Lindsay said. "As long as you're prepared to work hard, you're in."

"Oh, I'll work hard," she assured them. She'd wanted this for so long, and now it was finally hers.

"Okay then." Nathan shook her hand. "Why don't you get working on that ad for a new receptionist?"

"Thank you. I will." She returned to her desk and just sat for a minute, as the events of the morning finally sank in. She waited to feel happy and excited about her new job, but her churning stomach refused to settle down.

Patrick's angry words, his disappointed eyes, were all she could think about.

CHAPTER TWELVE

As PATRICK LEFT THE OFFICES of Fox & Fisher, he took no notice of the people around him, or the smells and noises of the city. Not even the weather, cold and damp, fazed him in the slightest.

He recognized that he was in a fog, but this was something he couldn't shrug off. When was the last time he'd been this angry? He couldn't remember, unless it was back when he was a kid, and he'd started to clue in to the fact that his father had a new life—and it didn't include him.

His father had been unemployed at the time the divorce with his mother went through. He'd agreed to send money when he could, and Patrick's mother had accepted this. Later, when his father became successful, she never considered fighting for regular support payments, never considered hiring a lawyer or going to court.

He remembered the pains his mother had taken each time economic straits had forced her to write his father for money for his schooling, for braces, for ski lessons. She'd never asked for anything she didn't consider essential—these were all things his half siblings took for granted. And she never took a nasty tone—he knew because he'd sometimes peeked at those letters.

But still, his father had made her account for every penny he sent, never seeming to consider that under the law she could have legitimately asked for much more.

Patrick had resented the hell out of his father then, but the anger he felt today was something different.

This time he was angry at *himself.*

How had he been so taken in by this woman? He'd been utterly deceived. He'd thought she was intelligent and hardworking, compassionate and beautiful in every sense of the word.

But she was just a pampered heiress, amusing herself by playing with other people's lives. He hoped her partners fired her for what she'd done. Not that it would matter to her. When regular people lost their jobs they had to worry about rent and grocery bills.

Nadine Kimble *Waverly* would have none of those concerns.

When he reached his apartment, Patrick slammed the door shut, then went to close all the blinds. Next, he made a pot of coffee, then set up his computer at the kitchen table.

He was one of those working stiffs who *did* need his paycheck…or in his case, his advance payment from his publisher. That meant he had to get his revisions done, which meant all this stuff about June and Stephen and Nadine had to be ignored for now.

Stephen. He wondered if he would have found his son sooner if he'd hired a real investigator. Would the situation have turned out any better?

Reluctantly, he had to admit he didn't think so.

He checked his message machine on the off chance that Stephen had been in touch while he was out. Nothing but a reminder notice from his dentist about an upcoming appointment.

Maybe he should make the first move. He wondered how Stephen would feel about a ski trip to the Alps. Patrick wasn't above using a little bribery to try and connect with the boy. Maybe he'd give Stephen another week to adjust to his existence, then give him a call and see how he felt about the idea.

Feeling marginally calmer now that he had a plan, Patrick fixed himself a cup of coffee, then powered up his computer. For the rest of the day he focused on his book and his revisions. He drank the entire pot of coffee, then made another. When he was hungry he ordered pizza.

For a week he worked as if words were his oxygen. Every waking hour he was pulling them out of the air and putting them down on paper. He fussed with this book as though it was the only thing on earth that mattered to him.

And when it was as perfect as he could make it, he sent it to his editor, then promptly fell into bed.

FRIDAY AFTERNOON, LINDSAY asked Nadine if she was free to attend an office meeting after work.

Nadine was surprised. Office meetings were usually in the morning. "Sure. Want me to pick up some refreshments?" For the morning meetings she usually bought bagels and cream cheese, but at this time of day she'd have to come up with something different. "I could order sushi."

"Already taken care of," Lindsay assured her before ducking back into her office. "By the way, since Kate is still on bed rest, the meeting is at her apartment."

"Okay." It felt strange not to be the one handling those sorts of details. Nadine supposed she would get used to it. There were lots of things she was going to need to adjust to.

She focused on the work Nathan had given her for the rest of the day, and at five Lindsay emerged from her office. "It's time to go. We're meeting Nathan there."

They took the subway and Lindsay chatted the entire way about a new case that was intriguing her. When they arrived at Kate's, Nadine was surprised to see that the apartment had been decorated with balloons and a cake was on the coffee table next to Kate's sofa.

"Congratulations!"

Was this a surprise baby shower? But why hadn't anyone told her so she could buy a gift? It took a few moments for the truth to sink in. Nadine turned to Lindsay. "This is for me?"

"Yes, you goof." Lindsay laughed and pulled her by the arm into the room. "We wanted to celebrate your official launch as a P.I.-in-training. We have bubbly and everything."

Nadine tried to say thank you, but she couldn't speak. She'd always felt a little apart from the others. Not only had she started as just the receptionist, but Kate, Lindsay and Nathan had all worked together at the Twentieth Precinct so they'd known each other for years. But now she truly was being accepted as a vital part of the team.

She wiped away a tear and managed to smile.

Jay handed out flutes of champagne and sparkling water, while Nathan cut the cake. Once everyone had their refreshments, Lindsay took the floor.

"Okay, the fun stuff is good, but we've got work to

do, as well. It's been a busy week. A crazy week. But we're going to survive this period of transition, I assure you. First, and most important, Kate, how did your appointment with your OB go today?"

"She gained almost a pound from last week," Jay said proudly.

"But the doc still insists on bed rest," Kate added glumly.

"They estimate the baby is still under six pounds." Jay topped up Kate's flute with sparkling water. "And it's only two weeks until our due date. Not much time to get bigger."

Kate smoothed her hands over the baby. "I'll be lucky to go two more weeks. The babe's in position and my cervix has started dilating. But what about your wedding plans? How are those coming? The invitations were lovely, by the way."

Nathan winked at Nadine.

"The alterations on my dress are done. But I still haven't found the right shoes." Lindsay glanced at Nadine, who felt terribly guilty. She'd promised Lindsay she would help her find a great pair of shoes.

"Everything else is in place," Nathan added. "We have food selected and flowers ordered."

"That's good." Kate stroked her swollen tummy. "It's hard to believe our baby will be almost a month old by then."

"It seems like everything is happening at once," Lindsay said. "Which brings us to the business portion of our meeting."

"First priority is hiring a new receptionist," Nathan said. "The employment agency is sending out a few candidates tomorrow."

"Wow, that was quick." Nadine hadn't thought she would be *that* easy to replace.

"The sooner the better. Lindsay and I were hoping you would spend mornings training your replacement, then afternoons working cases."

"That sounds fine. I have a lot I'll need to teach and explain." When Nadine had started at Fox & Fisher, she'd been working from scratch. She'd developed one system for filing reports, another for billing. She also had a long list of contacts to be used for everything from ordering office supplies to performing routine background checks. She'd be glad to pass along all this knowledge to the new person.

"Thanks, Nadine. Once the new receptionist is in place, you'll move into Kate's office." At Kate's raised eyebrows, Lindsay added, "Only until Kate has returned to work, or until we've negotiated more office space. That's on Nathan's list of things to do."

She turned to her fiancé, who nodded. "I have a meeting with the leasing agent next week."

"So," Lindsay concluded, "as you can see, we have busy times ahead. On Monday we'll meet in the boardroom and assign you your new cases."

Nadine nodded, anticipation rising like the bubbles in her champagne. She was going to have *cases*. It just sounded so *important*.

"In the meantime, I thought I should check—you've closed the file on the O'Neil case?"

Though Patrick was never far from her thoughts, the mention of his name was immediately sobering. She still wasn't satisfied with the way she'd handled the case, despite Lindsay's and Nathan's reassurances.

Diane hadn't answered her letter, so she didn't have a photo of Stephen on file. Plus, she hadn't been able to convince Patrick to do the DNA test.

But she'd found Stephen. That was the main thing.

"I've closed the file," she said. "And I sent out the final report and invoice last week. I hope you don't mind, but I ate some of my hours. I figured under the circumstances…" She glanced at her partners' faces and was relieved to see nods of approval.

"It's best we put that one behind us," Nathan agreed. "Now on to Kate's maternity leave—"

PATRICK SLEPT FOR TWELVE straight hours after meeting his deadline. When he woke at noon on Saturday, he felt an unusual lack of energy. Would anyone notice, would anyone care, if he didn't get out of bed?

Probably not. But years of honed discipline finally guilted him into throwing on his warmest running gear and heading out for some much needed exercise. Snow was falling as he paced himself lazily along the streets until he reached Central Park. He ran a short circuit, then continued back to his apartment where he showered, shaved and prepared to catch up with his life.

Only, did he have one?

A couple weeks' worth of mail was piled on his kitchen table again. All he did was stare vacantly into his coffee cup.

He knew people who lived on every major continent, from Asia, to Africa, to South America. If he wanted to organize a mountain-climbing expedition, he could have a team in place by midnight.

He was good at meeting women, too. Tonight he

could head out to a pub, find a pretty woman and convince her to have dinner with him. Tomorrow he'd probably wake up with her beside him in bed.

They'd go out for breakfast. And a few days later they'd go out again. The pattern would continue for a couple of weeks, until it was time to leave for his next book tour or to start research on his new book. He might call her a few times long distance. But the length of time between each call would grow longer and longer, until finally, he would see her name on his cell phone directory and not even be able to recall what she looked like.

A long time ago he'd chosen the life of a traveler. And he'd never regretted that choice.

Until now? Was that what this feeling was about right now...regret?

Patrick rubbed the side of his face—so smooth after his shave—and reached blindly into the pile of envelopes. The first one was from his publisher. He tore it open, then tucked the check into his wallet to be deposited later.

He reached for another envelope and was jolted out of his ennui by the sight of the return address: The Fox & Fisher Detective Agency. He ripped apart the manila folder and out slid a report and an invoice. He searched for a personal note from Nadine, but all that was attached was a printed slip folded over the report that said *Compliments of The Fox & Fisher Detective Agency.*

Tossing the package back to the table, he got up to pace, angry at first—didn't she at least owe him a brief personal message? Then, finally curious about what her report would say, he picked it up again.

He read it quickly once, then a second time more

closely. The report was very thorough, detailing every step of the investigation, beginning with the letter from June.

There was someone else he was angry at.

June's deception still ate at him. He'd had a right to know about the baby. He wouldn't have walked away from the obligation, knowing as he did the vital importance of a father in a boy's life. How dared she make that decision for him?

He set aside Nadine's report and took out June's letter for yet one more reading. He kept searching for answers that just weren't in there. Again, he wondered what had been in Stephen's letter. Maybe one day his son would trust him enough to tell him about it.

In the meantime, Patrick wondered who the mystery person was who had mailed the package in the first place. It didn't really matter, but she, or he, might have information about June's state of mind.

Who would June have trusted with her secret?

June's sister, Diane, was a likely candidate. Remembering that her phone number had been included in Nadine's report, he looked it up.

Without taking time to consider whether he was doing the smart thing, Patrick dialed her home phone number.

A woman answered. "Hello?"

"Is this Diane Stone?"

"Yes."

"This is Patrick O'Neil calling." He waited to see if she would remember.

"Well, well, Patrick O'Neil. After all this time…"

Her tone was so loaded, he realized she knew he was Stephen's father. Well, of course she knew. All of Diane's family would know. They'd met him several times.

"I gather you've heard about June?" she asked, her voice turning sober.

"Yes. I'm so sorry. I was in Alaska when the letter came, or I would have been at the funeral."

"Which letter are you referring to?"

Damn. He'd really hoped it had come from her. "I got back to the city about two weeks ago. I found a package in the mail—the return address was June's apartment in Chelsea. There was a letter from her to me in that package. She said she'd asked someone to send it to me after she passed on. I assumed that someone would be you."

"It wasn't." Diane sounded intrigued. "Do you mind if I ask what she had to say in her letter?"

"She told me that she'd had a son eighteen years ago. And that he was mine."

"You didn't know about Stephen?" She sounded scandalized.

"She didn't tell me. I was hoping you could explain why."

"Good Lord. I can't believe this. All these years... Hang on a minute, Patrick. I need to sit down."

Patrick realized he did, too. He sank back onto the kitchen chair and pushed aside his coffee, which was now cold.

A moment later, Diane began talking again. "This is so crazy. Did she offer any explanation for not telling you about your baby?"

"She said that she knew I was planning to travel after graduation and she didn't want me to feel trapped."

"That's it?"

"Yeah. And it isn't enough. I mean, she never even gave me a chance to do the right thing."

Diane was silent for a long while. "Does Stephen know this?"

"I hired an investigator to track him down. We found him working in a ski resort at Kicking Horse, British Columbia."

"So that's where he is. He hasn't phoned me once since he left. I'm afraid June's death has hit him hard. Is he okay?"

"I traveled to Canada to meet him. He's got a job at the ski hill at Lake Louise. We talked for a couple of hours, that was it. He seemed more confused than anything. Maybe he's working through his feelings about June's death. Or maybe he was just in shock at having a father turn up so unexpectedly."

"Well, I'm glad to hear that he's okay and he's working. Hopefully he'll contact us before too much longer." She let out a long sigh. "He looks a lot like his mother, doesn't he?"

"Yes, he does," Patrick replied, though he hadn't actually noticed. "Diane, I'd really like to figure out who mailed me that package. Do you have any ideas?"

"I suppose it could have been June's lawyer. Or maybe one of her friends. I'm sorry, Patrick, but she didn't tell me. I wish she had."

"Me, too."

"Maybe she felt too guilty. She let all of us assume you wanted nothing to do with the baby, you see. And she convinced us that it would be kinder to Stephen if we let him assume that you...you had passed on."

"That's a hell of a thing to find out now."

"It must be. I'm sorry. Listen—if you're talking to Stephen again, would you ask him to call me?"

He promised he would.

Then he went to the kitchen to make a fresh pot of coffee. As the water slowly dripped through the filter, he stared into space, rehashing his conversation with Diane.

She'd cleared up some of his confusion about the past, but the most important question still remained.

Why had June assumed he wouldn't—or couldn't— be a good father to Stephen? He wished he could have had the opportunity to ask her that in person.

CHAPTER THIRTEEN

THE PHONE AT THE RECEPTION desk was ringing. Ensconced in Kate's office on Wednesday afternoon, Nadine clenched the armrests of her chair and waited. *Come on, come on, what's taking so long?*

Finally Tamara Maynard answered, curtly, as if the call had interrupted something important. "Fox & Fisher."

Nadine gritted her teeth. Not one hour ago, she'd instructed Tamara to say, "Hello, this is The Fox & Fisher Detective Agency," in a pleasant, yet professional tone.

Nadine was not very impressed with the new receptionist, though she was trying to give her a chance. The hiring had happened very quickly. On Monday, four applicants had been sent to their office. Nathan and Lindsay had narrowed the choice down to two, then they'd asked for *her* opinion.

She'd chosen the one who seemed most desperate to get the job. Tamara Maynard was thirty-eight years old. She'd lost her position three months ago and was going to lose her apartment, too, she'd explained, if she didn't get another job soon. Her previous employer had discriminated against her because she was getting older. He liked young blondes in his office, which was what she had been nine years ago when he'd hired her.

Indignant on Tamara's behalf, Nadine voted for her, reasoning that since Tamara really needed the job she'd put in lots of effort.

Right?

Well, unfortunately it didn't seem to be working that way. She'd spent two mornings with Tamara so far, and all her patient instructions seemed to be for naught. Tamara hadn't exactly scoffed at her color-coded filing system, but Nadine had seen her flagrantly ignore it when she'd started several new client files later in the afternoon.

Fine for now, but wait until one of the investigators asked Tamara to pull all the cases to do with wrongful dismissal…then she'd wish she had cross-referenced the files in the first place.

"Nadine," Tamara called out. "Your new client is here."

Nadine winced at Tamara's cavalier approach. Was it too much to ask her to pick up the phone, rather than shouting across the hall?

At reception, Nadine found a white-haired lady using a walker standing uncertainly in front of Tamara's desk. Good Lord, Tamara hadn't even invited her to sit, or offered her a glass of water.

"Hello, Mrs. Waldgrave. It's a pleasure to meet you. Would you like coffee or water?"

"Do you have tea?"

"Of course. Tamara, would you bring a cup to the conference room, please? And let Nathan know that Mrs. Waldgrave is here."

"I was working on something else, but I guess I can put it aside for a minute."

Tomorrow, Nadine vowed, she would remind Tamara that it was a receptionist's job to *multitask*.

In the conference room she made certain Mrs. Waldgrave was comfortable before starting with a few general questions. After a minute, Nathan entered, bringing with him the cup of tea and a few packages of sugar and cream. Mrs. Waldgrave scorned those.

"Black tea is good enough for me."

Nathan raised his eyebrows, but made no other comment as he took a chair across from Nadine.

"As I mentioned on the phone," their new client said, her spine perfectly straight and her head held high, "I was cheated by a scoundrel and I'd like you to find him."

This was more like it, Nadine thought, turning to a new page in her notebook. *These* were the sorts of cases she had dreamed about solving.

"You told me you'd reported the fraud to the police," Nathan asked, his tone both kind and professional.

"That's right. Fat lot of good that will do. They told me to my face they probably wouldn't catch the cretin and even if they do, it's unlikely they'll recover my money. But it's not the four thousand dollars I care about. It's the principle of the thing. This man is going to target someone else—perhaps someone who can't afford the lost money as well as I—and I won't stand for it."

Nadine admired her backbone. "What was the scam?"

"About two months ago I received flowers from my grandson. It was my birthday, and I supposed he was too busy to bring them himself, so he had them delivered. Then all of a sudden last week, a man showed up at my door. At the time I thought I'd seen his face before, but I didn't immediately connect him to the flower deliveryman. It was so long ago, you see."

She was sharp as a tack, Nadine thought, scribbling along in her own modified shorthand.

"This man told me he was a friend of my grandson's. He seemed to know a lot about him. He said Michael was in trouble. He'd had a car crash, but no insurance and was too ashamed to come to me."

Mrs. Waldgrave shook her head wearily. "Well, with hindsight I feel so foolish. But Michael is my only grandchild. And he's done irresponsible things before. I told this man that I had an emergency stash on hand— and I got him what he needed."

"Which was the four thousand dollars?" Nadine asked.

"Yes."

Nathan's eyebrows went up. "It's probably not safe to keep sums that large in your home, ma'am."

"Yes. That's what the police said, too. But these days who's to say what is safer, the bottom of your freezer or a bank. At any rate, I told all this to the police. But I doubt very much they are going to find this character. Since I didn't have a withdrawal slip from a bank, I can't even prove my money is missing."

Nadine and Nathan asked her several more questions, before concluding the interview.

"We'll call you in a few days and let you know how the investigation is proceeding," Nadine promised as she walked the elderly lady out of the office and down to the street. After hailing her a taxi and helping her into the backseat, Nadine returned to her office.

Well, Kate's office, actually. Fortunately Kate was a very orderly person, so it had been easy to settle in. She'd apportioned a section of the credenza for her own files and had logged on as a guest user to Kate's computer.

Nadine was working on an action plan for Mrs. Waldgrave's case, to be reviewed by Nathan later, when Tamara called out her name again.

"Nadine. You have another client."

Nadine glanced at her day-timer, then her watch. She wasn't expecting anyone. She was just about to go out front to investigate, when someone appeared in her doorway.

It was Patrick.

She fell back into her chair, for the moment speechless.

Patrick raised his eyebrows in silent question, then taking her silence for acquiescence, entered the room.

During the past week, it seemed he had always been on her mind. She'd wished, so many times, that he would walk in the door. Even if he was still mad at her.

She studied his face, trying to judge his mood. "Did you get your revisions done in time?"

"One week early."

"Congratulations."

He was staring at her, but she couldn't read the expression in his eyes. "Have you heard from Stephen?"

"I've spoken to him, but he didn't call me. I called him. I suggested a ski trip to the Alps and he seemed open to the idea."

"That's wonderful." She was glad for Patrick. She knew that he needed to have some sort of relationship with his son, that in the long run it would make both him and Stephen happy. But why was he here? Where was this headed?

He didn't seem as angry as the last time she'd seen him, but he was reserved. Cautious.

"We also talked about college. Turns out he's not that

keen. But he does have an idea about a ski shop. I'm going to go over his business plan when we meet."

Warning bells sounded in her head. "Did he ask if you would invest?"

Patrick frowned. "What if he did?"

"It's just…I'm still worried that we didn't do the DNA testing."

"Would you give that a rest? If it makes you feel any better, I spoke to June's sister, Diane, the other day. She confirmed that I was Stephen's father. The whole family knew it."

Reluctantly, she gave in. "I guess there's no doubt then. Is that what you came here to tell me?"

"Actually, no. I received your report in the mail. And your invoice. It looks like you made a mistake."

Her spirits sank. Another one? She just wanted to close the book on this case and move on. "I guess you'd better sit down," she told Patrick, "and tell me the problem."

"THE MISTAKE IS WITH THE BILL," Patrick continued, handing her the invoice he'd received in the mail. "You've undercharged me. I know you put in a lot more hours than that."

She gave a sigh, then smiled, and he realized that she'd been worried it was something more serious.

He tried to hand her the check he'd filled in at home. "We had a deal. You fulfilled your end of it, and I want to stand by mine."

She wouldn't take it. "I've already spoken to the other partners about this. Under the circumstances… we're prepared to offer you a discount. Patrick, I may have found your son, but I was working under false pretenses. Believe me, I haven't stopped regretting what I did."

"But your strategy worked. You found my son and it looks like you've got the job you wanted. I've met the new receptionist. Congratulations on your promotion."

She swallowed, guilt darkening her eyes. "I'm working on cases under Nathan's supervision. I'm not a full partner, yet. More like an apprentice."

She hesitated, then asked, "Is—is that all you came here for? To talk about the bill?"

Good question. Why was he here? His own advice to himself had been to move on as quickly as possible. But he didn't think he could do that.

"I'm here because I can't forget you. Though, God knows I've tried." He'd gone to movies and bars, phoned up his buddies and had even started drafting notes for his new book.

No matter what he did, she was all he cared about.

"I've thought about you a lot, too." She sounded sincere as she said this, and he looked her square in the eyes.

For his own piece of mind he needed to find out if she really was the sweet, lovely woman he had taken her for…or just a rich socialite playing at private eye.

One thing he knew for sure. Last time they'd moved too fast. This time he wouldn't make that mistake.

"Do you have plans for this evening? Would you like to go out for dinner?"

Her eyes widened and color flooded her face. He'd surprised her. In a good way, he thought.

"I'd like that, Patrick. But I'm having dinner with my mom and dad tonight."

He'd come here, hoping to spend the evening with her and he wasn't keen on going home alone. "It's not how I pictured our first official date, but I must admit I'm curious to meet your parents. How do they feel about last-minute dinner guests?"

Nadine bit her lip, clearly torn. "Actually, they're not that good with it. They're kind of…formal people."

Maybe it wasn't fair, but he felt rejected by her response. A night with the parents had been a concession on his part. And now she was telling him he wouldn't be welcome.

But, of course, these weren't any parents. They were Wilfred and Sophia Waverly.

What a lot of baggage that sort of heritage entailed. Some men might find that kind of wealth and power alluring. He, frankly, wanted none of it.

"I'm free on Friday," Nadine offered.

Suddenly he wasn't sure any of this was a good idea. "Right. Well, I'll need to check my schedule. How about I give you a call?"

"Patrick. I'm sorry. I didn't mean to insult you. Please believe me when I say that a night with my parents would not be pleasant in any way."

"Who are you trying to protect? Them? Or me?"

"You, definitely. My mother and father are very loving parents. But they have old-fashioned ideas—"

She stopped, leaving him to fill in the blanks. "About the sort of men their daughter should date?"

"Well… I wouldn't have put it that bluntly. But—yes."

"Bloody hell, Nadine. How old are you?"

"Okay. I get your point. I'm an adult. That doesn't mean I stop loving and respecting my parents."

"To what point? Have you *ever* dated anyone your parents didn't consider 'appropriate'?"

"As it happens…no. But not because of my parents. I've just never wanted to." She swallowed, then looked him straight in the eye. "Until you."

He felt an instant desire for her then. A hot longing to reach across her desk and kiss her. But the price for this woman was just too high. He wasn't the sort of man to jockey for a position on anybody's social ladder.

"What about that guy you took to the Rain forest Charity Gala? Who was he? Where did you meet him?"

"Trenton works with my father. I—"

Color flooded her cheeks, making her even prettier. Yet the fact that she couldn't complete her sentence, only reinforced his opinion about her.

"I shouldn't have come here." He headed for the door, then paused and looked back at her. He wished he could stop himself from wanting her so much. "If you ever decide to stop letting your parents control your love life, give me a call."

NADINE SANK HER HEAD ONTO her desk. Well, that had gone just peachy, hadn't it? Maybe she should have cancelled her plans with her parents. But that was just the coward's way out.

What she *should* have done was invite Patrick to join her. The dinner would have been awkward, no one would have had a good time, but at least he would have known that she wasn't *ashamed* to be dating him.

She just didn't want to create *waves*.

Why get her parents in knots until she knew for certain that Patrick…

She closed her eyes as she remembered the way she'd felt when he walked into her office. Oh, she'd forgotten what a presence he had, what energy, what…raw, masculine appeal.

Unfortunately these attributes hadn't gone unnoticed by the new receptionist. Finally something had galvanized her enough to get up from behind her desk. Tamara appeared at Nadine's door, waving her hand as if she'd touched something hot.

"*Who* was *he?* Please tell me there's no company policy against dating the clients."

Nadine groaned and dropped her head again. What had she been thinking when she'd voted to hire this woman?

AN HOUR LATER, NADINE SENSED someone standing behind her. She turned from her keyboard and saw Lindsay scratching her head.

"What's wrong?"

"I need those files I was working on last week. You know the paternity cases?"

Nadine nodded. The same guy was being hit up by three different women for having fathered their children. The situation would have been ridiculous if it wasn't so sad.

"Can't Tamara find them?"

"Can Tamara find anything? Besides, it's after five. She was out of here at 5:01p.m."

"Hang on." Nadine hurried out to the reception area and located the files in question.

"Wonderful." Lindsay took a quick look to make sure they were the right files. Which, of course, they were. "You know, I'm glad we decided on that two-month trial period idea."

"It wasn't *we* who decided that, but *me*," Nathan pointed out. He locked his office for the night and pocketed the keys. "But Tamara's only been working here a few days. Give her a chance. And don't expect her to be another Nadine, 'cause that's not going to happen."

Nadine felt pleased that she was being held up as the gold standard where receptionists were concerned. She resolved to be more patient with Tamara tomorrow.

Lindsay stuffed the files into her leather bag, then met Nathan at the door where he helped her on with her coat.

"Coming, Nadine?" she invited. "We're going to the Stool Pigeon for dinner."

Nathan grimaced. The old-style English pub was not his favorite eating establishment, but he and Lindsay had worked out a deal where they went there once a week. Lindsay absolutely loved the people who owned the place, and their greasy, carb-loaded food.

Nadine sided with Nathan where pub food was concerned. Still, she would have said yes, if she hadn't had other plans.

"I'm going to work until six-thirty, then head straight to my parents'."

Nathan held the door open for Lindsay. "Okay, see you in the morning. You'll lock up?"

"You bet."

Once they were gone, the office fell into the strange, silent calm of after hours. Nadine hung around the reception desk for a bit. When she had worked there, she'd always tidied up at the end of the day. Tamara had done this, as well, but nothing was quite the way it should be, in Nadine's opinion.

She fought the urge to return a pen to the correct drawer and to straighten the papers in the in-basket. This was no longer her job. She had to learn to let go.

Finally she retreated to Kate's office—*her* office, though she was having trouble thinking of it that way.

Once she was behind the desk, she put aside the Waldgrave file she'd been working on and pulled out Patrick's.

She was bothered by what he'd said about his son. It made her uneasy that Stephen had broached the subject of money so soon. She *wished* she had been able to talk Patrick into that DNA test. She couldn't pinpoint why it felt so important. After all, he'd spoken to Diane and she'd been positive that Stephen was his son.

So why did she feel that something was wrong?

Nadine dove back into the file, rereading everything, starting with that first conversation with Diane. June's sister was the one who'd sent them in the direction of the Canadian Rockies. She'd said Stephen wanted a job on a ski hill, that he was traveling with a friend.

Stephen hadn't mentioned anything about his friend, though. Nadine wondered if they'd both been able to find jobs. Just as she was making a note to follow up on the friend, a new message popped into her in-box.

It was from Diane Stone.

Nadine opened it and read the short message.

It's funny that I opened your letter requesting Stephen's photo today, since I was just speaking to Patrick O'Neil on the phone a few days ago. It sounds like my big sister has left a bit of a mess behind her. I'm attaching a couple of photos. One of June and Stephen together, then another just of Stephen. I hope this helps.

Nadine opened the first attachment and froze at the photo of Stephen. He had red hair, a shade lighter than Patrick's reddish-brown, as well as his mom's high cheekbones and fine features.

Even allowing for a bad dye job, he wasn't the boy they had met in the lounge at Lake Louise.

He was the ski instructor she'd taken lessons from at Kicking Horse.

CHAPTER FOURTEEN

NADINE WAS TEMPTED TO BEG OUT of the evening with her parents, but she'd missed dinner last week due to her trip to Canada, and her parents were already resentful enough about her job at Fox & Fisher.

So after she'd locked up the office for the night, she hailed a cab and gave the driver her family's Madison Avenue address.

Along the way, she pulled out her cell phone. She didn't want to call Patrick. She felt too humiliated after their last conversation.

But she had to tell him. As soon as possible.

She hit the call button, then waited, holding her breath, for him to answer. When the call went through to voice mail, she couldn't decide if she was relieved or disappointed.

"This is Nadine. I know you're upset with me, but I've just found out something important about Stephen. I'm going to drop by your place later, around ten o'clock. If that's too late, leave me a message and we'll set something up for tomorrow."

She was still boggled by what she had discovered. It had been such an audacious trick. What had Stephen hoped to accomplish? And how was Patrick going to react when he found out the truth?

She tucked her phone back into her purse as the cab pulled up to the five-story mansion where she'd grown up, just a block from Central Park. Her bedroom was one of four on the top story and sometimes when she spent the night—for Christmas and other special occasions—she could remember how she'd felt as a child, isolated and lonely, wishing for nothing more than to be an ordinary, average child, living an ordinary, average life.

If she stayed in the family home for too long, those old feelings would creep back into her psyche, but this was just a quick visit, and she was happy to see the family's long-standing housekeeper when she opened the main door.

"Hi, Martha. How are you?" She handed her a package with the gifts she'd purchased in Lake Louise. "I brought you a little something when I was in Canada last week."

"You always are the sweetest thing." Martha's skin was wrinkled now, but her smile was warm as ever. She peeked into the bag and exclaimed over the gifts. Then she took Nadine's coat. "Your parents are waiting for you."

Following the sound of her father's favorite Oscar Peterson recording, Nadine passed through the foyer into the music hall. Her heels clicked on the marble floors and her gaze skimmed past the impressive grand piano where she'd learned to play "Chopsticks," but not much else, as a child.

Her parents were seated next to the fireplace. Their clothing, her mother in a dress and emeralds, her father in a suit and tie, made the skirt and cashmere sweater she'd worn to work seem casual.

She kissed her parents and accepted her glass of kir

royal. Dinner at her parents' followed a predictable routine. Cocktails in the music hall, followed by a three-course meal in the dining room, and ending with dessert and coffee in the library.

She'd grown up this way. While the drawn out meal, the formal dress and manners had been stifling to her as a child, over the years she'd grown accustomed to her parents' ways.

But tonight she found herself seeing everything through Patrick's eyes—or how she imagined he would see it. She could picture the ironic twist his mouth would take as he observed her world, and her family, from his own small-town, New England perspective.

"So, darling," her mother said, "fill us in on the past few weeks. How was your trip to Canada?"

"So much happened, I hardly know where to begin. For one thing, I'm no longer receptionist. I've been promoted to junior investigator."

She hadn't expected them to be pleased, and judging from their flat expressions, they weren't. Before they could express any negative reactions, she pressed on.

"And I've met someone," she blurted, before she lost her nerve. "His name is Patrick O'Neil. He spoke at the Charity Gala a few weeks ago."

Her father frowned. "Was that the Children's Wish Foundation?"

"No, dear. Amazon rain forests." She turned to her daughter, eyes narrowed. "As I recall you left early, Nadine. Even before dinner. How did you have the opportunity to meet Patrick O'Neil?"

It was too soon to tell the whole story, about Patrick being her first client and how she found his son. For now she'd be smart to keep the story simple and brief. "Patrick was one of the few people I managed to speak with before I had to run."

"Well."

As her parents exchanged a long look, Nadine sipped her drink and wondered how to proceed from here. Then, without any forethought, she found herself adding, "I was thinking of inviting him to dinner. Here. Next week. So you could meet him."

"We've already met him," her father said drily. "At the gala. I hardly think we need to meet again. Now, if your relationship should become *serious*—which it can't possibly be after just a few weeks—we'll obviously issue him an invitation."

"It won't come to that." Her mother smoothed a wrinkle from her silk skirt. "You're young and you want to have fun. But Patrick O'Neil isn't the sort of man you settle down with."

"Oh, Mom. Why do you and Dad always have to sound like you're characters in a Jane Austen novel? This is the twenty-first century."

"Nadine, I know you find it tiresome, but the Waverlys have a long proud history in this country," her mother said. "And you are our only heir. You've decided to play at being a private detective…and we've come to terms with that."

"But one day," her father continued, "you're going to be required to sit on the board of directors at Waverly Corporation and the Endowment Foundation. You'll be the custodian of assets and traditions that must be preserved and passed on to future generations."

It was such an old argument between them, that no

one raised their voices. Nadine didn't even bother to reply. She'd say nothing more right now. She'd introduced the subject and that was enough for now.

WHEN PATRICK MADE IT HOME after a solo dinner at his favorite Indian restaurant, he didn't know what to make of the message from Nadine.

She said she had something important to tell him. But what could that possibly be? To him, the promise of news sounded like an excuse.

Maybe she wanted to squeeze in a little action after dinner with her folks.

In his dreams. No, in *her* dreams. After this afternoon, he was *done* with this woman.

Nevertheless, he put on some music and tidied up his apartment. He was washing dishes when she arrived. He stopped, dried his hands, then answered the phone. After pressing the code to let her through the security door, he went to the hall to meet her.

She was dressed in the same outfit she'd been wearing earlier. But now she looked tired. And worried. She tucked her hair behind her ears as she gazed at him.

"Come in. I'm not going to bite." But as she walked past him, he deliberately moved so that her shoulder brushed against his chest. She hesitated, then kept going.

He watched as she sized up his place. He had a lot of square footage for a Manhattan co-op. Big windows. A nice view. Of course, it wouldn't seem like much to someone with her background. "So, princess, how was dinner at the royal court?"

She flinched.

It was a low blow and he was ashamed of himself. "Want a drink?"

She murmured, "No thanks," but he went ahead and poured a few inches of Scotch for himself.

"So." With his gaze still fixed on her, he lifted the glass to his mouth and took a fortifying swallow. "You have something to tell me?"

She lifted her chin. "I told my parents about you tonight."

"What?"

"I told them—I'd met someone. You. They remembered you, of course."

This was the last thing he'd expected her to say. But it was much too little and much too late. "Sweetheart, I'm not sure why you bothered."

He'd wounded her with that, and again he felt vaguely guilty rather than satisfied. He took another swallow of the Scotch, annoyed at himself for letting her get to him, even now.

"Yes. Well, maybe I shouldn't have said anything. But I did."

"And now they're dying to meet me?"

When she glanced away from him, he laughed. "Not hardly, huh? Well, you called it, didn't you? So what brings you here so late, Nadine? Looking for a little tequila sunrise on the wrong side of town?"

"Stop it. I have something important to tell you and it isn't going to be easy." She opened her purse and pulled out a piece of paper. "I printed this at the office. The resolution could be better, but it's clear enough, I think."

She passed it to him, and he took a look.

"Who's this?"

She sighed, then removed a second piece of paper. "This is a photo of him with his mother."

Again he accepted the paper, only this time he felt a jolt of surprise. "That's June." It was a bigger, clearer photograph than the one printed with her obituary and he felt a pang for how her disease had aged her.

"Look at the boy beside her."

"Why? It isn't Stephen."

Nadine didn't say anything.

He stared at the photo again. First June. Then the boy. Slowly he straightened and faced Nadine. "The kid we met at Lake Louise… He wasn't Stephen Stone."

She shook her head. "No."

"Then who was he?"

"I'm guessing he's someone who knew Stephen. Maybe the friend he traveled out with."

Patrick was filled with a weary dismay. Those four days spent in Canada had been a bloody waste of time. "So we're back to square one."

"Not exactly."

He went still. "Oh?"

"I believe I met the real Stephen Stone at the Kicking Horse Resort. When he heard who I was, and why I was looking for him, he pretended that he was a substitute instructor and that Stephen had just left the resort to go work at Lake Louise."

"That's crazy."

"Is it? From the start, you guessed that your son's first reaction would be anger. He didn't want to meet you, so he asked a buddy of his to pretend to be him."

"Why bother? All he had to do was deny being Stephen and wait for us to leave."

"Maybe he was worried you wouldn't let it drop until you'd found *someone* you thought was your son. Or maybe he was curious. Maybe he wanted to know what you were planning to say."

"Following along with that logic, I suppose his buddy tried to dye his hair red, since that's Stephen's most recognizable characteristic."

"Yes. The color ended up closer to purple than red, but it succeeded in hiding his true hair color, which was all he really needed to do."

"Bloody hell. I can't believe this." Patrick started to pace, then stopped. Nadine's theory fit the facts, but it was far from palatable. What a nasty trick the kid had played.

But could he really blame him? He thought about how angry he had felt toward his own father. Once, when he'd been visiting the new family, his father's wife had bragged about how her husband had never missed one of their rug rats' baseball games.

Patrick had acted as if he couldn't care less, but inside he had burned. His father had never once made it to any of his sporting events.

Just as Patrick had never been there for Stephen. What he needed to make sure Stephen understood, though, was that he hadn't been given a choice. He was as much a pawn in this game as his son had been.

"I guess we would have avoided this mess if I'd taken that damn DNA test you were always pushing on me."

To her credit, she didn't rub it in. "It's not too late. I'm planning to fly back to Canada as soon as possible and finish this properly."

"You mean, *we're* flying back to Canada."

By now she knew him too well to argue. "Hopefully

Stephen is still working at the Kicking Horse Resort. He's had some time to process your appearance in his life. Maybe by now he'll be genuinely interested in meeting you."

"Right." Patrick didn't think it was going to be as easy as that. "I wouldn't let him know we were coming just in case. And what do we do about the imposter?"

"Let's wait and see what Stephen has to say first. He may not realize his buddy was trying to extort money from you."

"And if he does?"

"Then maybe he was even angrier than you thought."

THE NEXT MORNING NADINE WAS waiting at the coffee station when Lindsay and Nathan arrived for work. Since Tamara wasn't due for another fifteen minutes, she had put on the first pot of the day, knowing that her partners were going to need the caffeine. Especially after what she had to tell them.

As soon as they were out of their coats, she handed them each a full mug.

"Oh, no," Lindsay said, accepting the beverage gratefully. "What's wrong now?"

"I've got good news and bad news. Which do you want first?"

At the exact same time Lindsay said, "Bad," and Nathan said, "Good."

"Okay." Nadine leaned against the corner of her—Tamara's—desk. "Let's start with bad. I have to travel to Canada again. We found the wrong son."

"What do you mean?" Lindsay asked, while Nathan looked equally confused.

Nadine explained how she'd discovered that the boy they'd met at Lake Louise was not June Stone's son—and therefore not Patrick's, either. Then she put out her theory…and they were both impressed.

"Well done, Nadine. I think you're right," Nathan said slowly.

"Of course she's right. If only the client had agreed to take that stupid DNA test…" Lindsay grabbed a handful of her own hair, frustrated. "I hate to lose you here at the office, especially when it's Tamara's first week."

"Patrick's making the travel arrangements. He probably won't have plans in place until the weekend. In the meantime I'll get as much done here as I can. Which brings me to the good news…"

"Spill," Nathan said. "You look as excited as a kid at Christmas."

"I spent a lot of time on the Waldgrave case yesterday. I started by visiting the florist shop where that deliveryman worked. When I told the owner that we suspected her deliveryman was using her clients for his con operation, she agreed to cooperate with my investigation."

Lindsay and Nathan both looked impressed.

"She told me that Ted Isaac works full-time, but that he has all-day Sunday and Thursday mornings off. That got me thinking…morning is probably the perfect time for him to run his scams. Not very many people have visitors on Thursday morning, so he'd have a good chance of catching his victims at home and alone."

"Did I tell you she had a good head on her shoulders, or what?" Nathan grinned. "Since this is Thursday, I think I know where you're heading with this."

"Yes, I have to follow him."

"I'm all for that," Lindsay said. "But I'm not keen on you going out alone."

"Me, either. Unfortunately I have a meeting at ten that I can't get out of," Nathan said regretfully.

"I'm busy, too. You'll have to tail him next week, Nadine."

"And meanwhile another innocent victim is cheated out of his or her hard-earned money?"

In the end Lindsay and Nathan agreed that she could perform the surveillance as long as she promised not to approach the man under any circumstances and to abort the mission if her cover got blown.

Nadine changed into the gym pants and jacket she'd brought along from home. Then she tied her hair into a ponytail and slid on a cap and a pair of sunglasses.

"Wear a warm sweater under that jacket," Nathan said, offering last-minute advice. "It's supposed to snow."

"Oh, yuck."

"Snow is actually a good thing," he told her. "You can disguise yourself with a big scarf and hat without looking conspicuous."

As Nadine packed binoculars and a video camera into a backpack, she could feel the smile on her face growing wider and wider.

Her dream was finally coming true and she couldn't believe how great it felt. She truly was a private detective. She was going to get this guy and protect innocent senior citizens. Talk about job satisfaction.

CHAPTER FIFTEEN

PATRICK WAS BOOKING PLANE tickets to Calgary when his editor called. He hit the confirmation button to conclude his transaction, then swiveled his chair so he could face the view.

It was four weeks before Christmas and winter had arrived with a vengeance. The tops of the tallest buildings were hidden from view, as the great city was muffled by a major dump of snow. Six inches they were forecasting.

Then sunshine tomorrow.

He hoped they were right. He wanted clear skies by Friday, since he was desperate to get back to the Rocky Mountains and see the real Stephen. To get snowed in at the airport would be the ultimate frustration.

"Hey, Oliver. Sorry for that delay. I was just in the process of finalizing some travel arrangements. Have you looked at the revised manuscript?"

"I have and I love it. The Alaska book is ready for the copy editor, which brings me to the next matter of business. Your press tour for the New Zealand book."

"How many cities?" Public appearances and book signings were the least favorite part of his job, but he tried not to complain. Every year his sales figures were climbing, and if he wanted to keep writing for a living, that was an important trend to maintain.

Oliver went over the details of the trip, which was scheduled for five weeks, with a three-day break over the holidays. "Then in the new year it'll be time to start another book. Have you picked a subject?"

"I'm thinking extreme mountain sports in the Canadian Rockies. How does that sound?"

"Hmm. Could be good. Especially if you can squeeze in a dramatic encounter with a grizzly."

"I'd rather not. I love a good adrenaline rush, but I'm not stupid."

"You jump out of airplanes, Patrick, so that point is somewhat debatable."

"I jump out of airplanes, wearing a parachute. That's an important distinction. And one of these days, you're coming with me." Patrick smiled, trying to imagine the academic Oliver leaping out into midair at thirteen thousand feet.

"Like hell, I will. But back to business. When you get the time, send me a proposal for the Rocky Mountain book. Meanwhile, I'll get working on the contract with your agent."

"Sounds good, Oliver." Patrick disconnected the call. Five years ago, he would have been exuberant about a new book contract. Now he signed up for the next project casually, as a matter of course.

The same went for his traveling. He remembered when just the prospect of visiting a new part of the world had filled him with joy. He had lived from adrenaline rush to adrenaline rush, carefully managing risk in exchange for maximum highs.

Not having a wife or children had been a conscious choice on his part. He figured it wouldn't be fair to them, given his lifestyle. And he had never minded coming home to an empty apartment at the end of his exploits. Not as long as he knew that another adventure beckoned in the near future.

That was how his life had worked for many years now. But this time he felt different. His apartment had a hollow quality he'd never noticed before. Rather than dreaming of ideas for his next book, he found himself thinking about June and Stephen and trying to imagine what their lives had been like without him.

And he thought about Nadine, much as he didn't want to.

He pictured her in the various rooms of his home. Sitting on the kitchen counter talking to him while he cooked. Curled up on the leather sofa beside him watching the news. Naked in his bed....

Patrick groaned. Damn it, she was too complicated for him, but somehow she'd bewitched him. And he didn't know what in the hell he was going to do about it.

AT FOUR O'CLOCK ON THURSDAY afternoon, Nadine was counting out money at her desk when she became aware that she was being watched. She looked up.

Nathan was standing by the door, holding a pile of papers and wearing his reading glasses. Lindsay thought they made him look sexy. Nadine's vote was for cute.

Sexy was a term that applied to only one man, in her opinion.

Patrick had looked so hot when she'd stopped by his place. He'd come to the door in a dark T-shirt that hugged his great physique and jeans that rode low on his hips. His hair had been tousled in a way that had nothing to do with fashion, and he'd had a one-day growth that suited his rugged features.

He had looked so damn *good*.

But it wasn't just his looks that attracted her. It was something deeper, the raw, masculine side of him that pulled at her. Even when he was angry or distant, she could still feel the embers of desire, waiting for the slightest waft of oxygen to roar into flame.

"Nadine? What are you doing?"

She stopped daydreaming and looked down at her hands. "I'm putting hundred-dollar bills into an envelope."

Nathan laughed. "Yeah. But why? I've got to tell you, it doesn't look good."

She put the last of the money inside, sealed the envelope, then set it aside. "I spent the day tracking down the Flower Con Man, Nathan. With all the snow, it wasn't fun, but I've got statements from two of his victims, now—Mrs. Waldgrave and another elderly woman named Daisy Proctor. I also have pictures of the con man taking money from Daisy and a written statement from the owners of Flouting Flowers proving that he had delivered flowers to both Mrs. Waldgrave and Mrs. Proctor several months prior to conning them out of money."

"That's amazing."

Nadine picked up a second envelope, thicker than the first. "All the evidence is in here. I have an appointment at five-thirty with the officer who took Mrs. Waldgrave's original statement. Hopefully this will be enough to allow the police to make an arrest."

"Very impressive. But you still haven't explained about the money."

Her smile faded. "I spent about an hour talking to Mrs. Proctor. She isn't in the same situation as Mrs. Waldgrave. She was conned out of five thousand dollars that she simply can't afford to lose. You should see her apartment, Nathan. It's tiny and bare-bones. But she has a dog, a little Yorkie named Goliath."

"Cute."

"I swear, that Yorkie weighs more than Mrs. Proctor. I think she scrimps on meals for herself so she can afford his food and vet bills."

Nadine tucked the two envelopes into her briefcase. "I'd better get going. The police precinct where we're meeting is on the Upper East Side."

"Wait a minute. You still haven't explained. That money. Who does it belong to? Did you somehow get it from the Flower Con guy?"

"No. It's my money."

"But—" He removed his glasses and stared at her. "Are you planning to give that to Mrs. Proctor?"

"I'll just slide the envelope under the door. She'll never know where it came from."

He shook his head. "Nadine. You can't do that."

"Why not?"

"In this job you're going to run across a lot of people who are down on their luck. We can't help all of them. It just isn't possible."

She understood what he was saying and why. But in this case he was wrong.

"I've told you about my family, so you won't be surprised to find out that I have a trust fund. It's more money than I'll need in my lifetime…so what better use for it than to help people like Mrs. Proctor?"

"There are charitable foundations—"

"Sure. And my family makes donations to lots of them. And we attend galas and go to silent auctions and sit on committees. But this is different. It's important to me to do this, to help this one individual woman who has fallen through the cracks."

"Jeez, Nadine. You are something else. I had something to talk to you about, but it can wait until tomorrow. You've got more important things to do right now."

NADINE WAS CHILLED FROM the tips of her toes to the hair follicles on her head, when she arrived home a little past nine in the evening. She shook the remaining snow from her boots and hung up her cashmere coat. The message light on her phone was flashing and she made a mental note to call her mother after she'd unwound with a glass of wine and a soak in her tub.

But she'd no sooner settled into the warm water, than her phone started ringing and she realized she'd made a tactical error.

If she'd called her mother *first* there wouldn't have been any interruptions to her nice bath.

She pressed the speaker button on the intercom system her parents had had installed for her when she'd first moved in. It was a phone and security system all wrapped up in one nifty bit of technological wizardry. "Hi, Mom, I'm sorry I didn't call sooner but it's been a crazy day."

There was a pause. Then a familiar, deep voice replied, "Tell me all about it, sweetheart."

Nadine cringed. "Sorry about that. I thought you were my mom. Obviously."

"I may not be who you thought I was. I'm still willing to listen."

The low timbre of his voice brought back hot, sweet memories of their night together. She slid lower into the tub until all that was exposed was her head from the chin up. "I'm sure you didn't call to hear about my day."

"What's that sound in the background?"

She went very still.

"Are you in the bath?"

She couldn't say yes. She couldn't talk to him, knowing he was picturing her naked. She tried to stand up silently, but it was impossible. The water sloshed—he'd be sure to hear.

"Hang on a second." She shoved the phone into a plush towel to muffle the noise, then stepped out to the bath mat and grabbed her robe.

Even with the fabric wrapped tightly around her body, she still felt exposed as she picked up the phone again.

"Okay. I'm back."

"Why did you get out of the tub? I don't have special powers. I couldn't see you." He paused. "Though I wish I could."

Her body tingled, as if he were here in this room with her. Watching her. Reaching out for her.

She left the bathroom, walking along polished hardwood, to the bedroom. As soon as she saw her plush duvet, she pictured Patrick lying there, waiting for her.

She closed her eyes.

"I solved a case today," she said. "I stopped a man who was conning elderly women out of thousands of dollars."

"Congratulations."

He really sounded impressed and she could feel herself smiling. "How was your day?"

"My editor offered me a new book contract."

"Wow. That's exciting. You must be thrilled."

"Once upon a time I would have been. Now I find it just, I don't know. Satisfying, I suppose."

He sounded tired, she thought. "Maybe you're preoccupied by Stephen."

"That's true enough. And you've reminded me why I called. I wanted to let you know I booked our travel arrangements. Are you okay to leave Saturday morning at eight?"

"Sure. That gives me one more day to clear things up at the office."

"Good. I figured we fly into Calgary, rent a car and drive straight to Kicking Horse. I've booked us two rooms for the night."

"Okay." Nadine swallowed. It was hard not to think about another mountain resort, the one at Emerald Lake. She and Patrick had ended up there by accident, thanks to that avalanche. What had happened between them that night had probably been an accident, too.

Something she had to put behind her. Something she *would* put behind her.

This trip would not be like the last one. There would be no long conversations, no stolen romantic evenings. Only work.

"I was thinking about that kid who pretended to be Stephen," Patrick said. "I realized I gave him June's letter."

Her stomach tightened. "That's right. You did. I hope he passed it along to Stephen."

"What if he didn't? If he's the kind of guy to extort money, then he might not care too much about passing on a letter. Damn, I really should have listened to you about that DNA testing."

"Don't worry about it now," she advised. "Wait until we actually meet with Stephen. For all we know, he already has the letter from his mom."

THE WEATHER FORECAST PROVED accurate and the snow-storm was long gone by the weekend. Patrick had insisted that he pick up Nadine on the way to the airport this time and he wasn't surprised when the cab stopped in front of an aristocratic-looking apartment building. A uniformed doorman emerged first, with a suitcase that Patrick recognized as Nadine's.

She followed right behind the doorman with her brief-case strapped over her shoulder, wearing the same stylish ski jacket, fur-lined boots and hat as on the previous trip.

With hindsight he wondered how he hadn't guessed she came from money from the beginning. Her tony address was just the tip of the iceberg. A regular P.I. couldn't afford to dress the way she did. And those excellent manners, even her graceful way of walking…all were the product of a certain, privileged kind of background.

He felt a draft of cold air as the driver opened the back door for her and the scent of her perfume greeted him before her words. "Good morning."

He grunted in reply. He almost wished she'd kept him waiting so he'd have an excuse for his bad temper. All night long he'd tortured himself with the image of her soaking in her bathtub. He'd pictured her stepping out of the tub, her body glistening with moisture.

He'd wanted to be there, to lick away every drop that was lucky enough to cling to her skin.

Good God. He was going to drive himself insane if he continued to think this way.

Condensation had formed on the side windows, and as they drove away, he swiped it clean so he could look at passing scenery that held no interest for him.

"It's a big day, isn't it? Just think…in about ten hours we should be at the Kicking Horse Resort."

His stomach tightened around an emotion he was used to feeling before he did something physically challenging, or potentially dangerous, like jumping off a cliff with a hang glider.

Tonight, if all went well, he'd meet Stephen. The *real* Stephen.

What would it be like, seeing his son, in person, for the first time? Would it be anticlimactic and awkward like that staged meeting with the imposter in Lake Louise? Or would he feel something real?

He felt even more nervous about meeting Stephen than he had the first time. He wasn't sure why. Maybe because now he knew Stephen wanted nothing to do with him.

He shifted positions and Nadine glanced at him sympathetically. For some reason he resented the fact that she seemed to understand what he was going through. He turned away again and didn't say another word until they were at the airport.

"I have our boarding passes on my BlackBerry," he told her as they stepped out to the sidewalk and grabbed their bags.

"Did you check if the flight is on time?"

About a dozen times. "It is."

He set a fast pace, but she managed to keep up with him as they made their way past the line ups for tickets, boarding passes and luggage drop-off. After they'd cleared airport security, Nadine stopped at a newsstand, while he paced in front of their gate, keeping an eye on the departure time.

LaGuardia was famous for having a high percentage of delayed flights, but fortunately, today, theirs wasn't one of them.

The trip to Toronto passed quickly enough with him and Nadine silently passing back and forth the various sections of the *Times*.

The next leg of the trip was more problematic. The flight to Calgary was almost four hours long. As he watched Nadine pull a couple of magazines from her briefcase, he realized he hadn't thought to bring along any reading material. Last time he'd passed the time working on his manuscript.

But he hadn't even brought his laptop on this trip. And the damned seats seemed even more uncomfortable than usual. He couldn't decide whether it was better to keep his chair reclined or upright.

About an hour into the trip Nadine glanced at him and sighed. She handed him her copy of *The New Yorker*.

He flipped through it, but only a couple of the articles interested him. The short story was strange and he didn't like the ending.

Half an hour later, he must have been fidgeting again, because Nadine gave him an exasperated look. "I've always liked the Proust Questionnaire…want to give it a whirl?"

"I suppose you need an Ivy League education to know what a Proust Questionnaire is."

She rolled her eyes. "It's just a bunch of questions— an old parlor game, really. It's published at the back of every *Vanity Fair.*" She turned to the last page of the magazine in her hands. "Here's the first question— What is your idea of perfect happiness?"

He instantly flashed back to the day he and Nadine had gone skiing at Lake Louise. Those two stolen hours of pure pleasure. "Standing on the top of a mountain with the sun beating on my back and a hill of powder in front of me." He stopped there, not adding the fact that she was with him. Her presence had only been incidental, anyway.

"Nice." She smiled then glanced at the next question. "What is your—"

"Hold on." He remembered the feeling he had at the end of their last trip. That she knew so much about him, and he so little about her. That had turned out to be so true.

It was time to even the scales.

"What's *your* idea of perfect happiness?"

She only paused for a second to think. "Doing something that helps another human being, without worrying about a personal reward."

"Really?"

She hesitated, then said, "That case I told you about the other day? A young man was conning elderly people—mostly women—out of thousands of dollars. I gathered enough evidence for the police to arrest him. Not only that, but I managed to—recover—the money he'd stolen from one of the women."

He was floored. "That's amazing."

"It felt fantastic, Patrick. It really did."

He stared at her, transfixed as much by her smile, as by her story. When he'd found out about her heritage and her wealth and her formal job title, he'd tried to convince himself that she was just an heiress amusing herself by pretending to be a private detective.

But that had been unfair. She did care about her job. She definitely cared about the people she worked for. And she worked hard.

She'd lied to him about some pretty important facts, but at heart she was the same sweet, lovely person he'd thought she was.

And he was dangerously close to falling in love with her.

CHAPTER SIXTEEN

THEY ARRIVED AT KICKING HORSE Resort shortly after seven in the evening. They'd driven through the avalanche zone without incident this time. Patrick's growly mood had softened after the Proust Questionnaire and now Nadine guessed that his silence was due only to the proximity of his son and their upcoming meeting.

While he set about registering for their rooms and collecting the door keys, she inquired with the concierge after Stephen. There was a separate residence for employees who lived on-site. She was told he might be there, or he might have gone into the town of Golden for the evening.

She was just concluding that it would be easier and more practical to set up a meeting in the morning, when three young men entered the lodge. They were chatting easily, like friends who were comfortable together and knew one another well. And they were dressed in street clothes, not ski gear, so it was easy to spot Stephen with his red hair and his mother's high cheekbones.

He spied her right away, too, and from the flush that immediately stained his face, she knew he'd remembered her.

He stopped where he was. "I need to check something," he said to his buddies. "I'll catch up with you later."

The other guys, one taller, one stouter, sensed nothing amiss and continued on their way through the lobby, their conversation picking up where it had left off, making plans for which room they would meet in to drink beers and hang out.

Stephen took a few steps in her direction. He hadn't spotted Patrick, who was speaking to a desk clerk right behind him, and so far Patrick hadn't seen him, either.

"You're back," Stephen said.

"I was hoping for a proper introduction this time." She held out her hand. "I'm Nadine Kimble, a private investigator from New York City."

He took a deep breath, then accepted the handshake. "I guess you've already figured out, I'm Stephen Stone."

At the sound of that name, Patrick turned. His gaze met Stephen's. The boy seemed to know who he was. Maybe he'd checked his father's name on the Web and found the author photos. Or maybe it was instinct.

Patrick said something quick to the clerk then walked toward them. He had his eyes on Stephen and nothing else. He went right up to him and grasped the boy by the shoulders.

With his gaze locked on Stephen's, he spoke in a voice filled with both wonder and certainty. "You're my son."

And his eyes, and Stephen's, filled with tears.

"THIS IS NO PLACE FOR A PROPER conversation," Patrick said, gathering his composure and taking charge of the situation. "Let's go to the lounge and have a drink."

"The one upstairs is quieter," Stephen offered.

"I think I'll head to my room first and freshen up," Nadine said.

She was being diplomatic, Patrick suspected. Trying to give them some time alone. But he wanted her with him. It would take the two of them to sort this mess out. "Why don't you come along and order something to eat. It's been a long time since that sandwich in Canmore."

She studied his face, then nodded. "Okay."

They found a table near the back of the room, far from the jazz pianist who was performing standards to a group of about fifteen customers.

During the amount of time it took to get settled in their seats, Stephen's body language had changed. He slouched into a chair and crossed his arms over his chest. Patrick realized what had happened.

They'd caught him off guard in the lobby, but he'd had time to lock his defenses back into place.

Patrick prayed for inspiration to say the right thing. Because this was big. This was as big as it got. Meeting that kid in Lake Louise had been a joke. He'd felt nothing because there was nothing to feel.

But all it had taken was one look at Stephen to *know*.

What got to him the most were the eyes. Stephen had Patrick's mother's eyes. Pale green and watchful. Windows to the soul? If so, Patrick could see hurt, as well as anger. Again he called upon his own memories as a boy who'd been disappointed by his father.

Those wounds, the deep, old kind, took time to heal.

He sensed Nadine watching him and turned. She gave him an encouraging smile and her intent gaze seemed to assure him that he was capable of handling this situation.

Stephen ended up being the first to speak. "So what's the story? Did Zach blow it or something?"

"Is that the name of the kid who impersonated you?"

Stephen twisted his head in an ambiguous motion.

"'Cause that was some nasty trick."

"Hey. What do you expect, showing up out of the blue with a private investigator?" He turned to Nadine. "No offense. You seem like a nice lady."

"Finding you wasn't easy, Stephen," she said. "That's why your father hired our agency to help him."

"Well, maybe I didn't want to be found. Ever think of that?"

Patrick had expected the boy to be angry. What he hadn't expected was that it would cause him so much pain to see his son suffering.

Stephen was right. What did he need with a father at this age? He'd been better off the way he was. Patrick started to stand, but Nadine put her hand over his.

"Now that you two are finally in the same room, why don't you at least hear each other out? This is what your mother wanted, after all."

Stephen fixed his pale eyes on Patrick. "Is that why you're here? Because she died?"

"I came because of her letter, yes. And I came because I wanted a chance to tell you—" His voice broke. Embarrassed, he started again, "To tell you that I'm here if you need anything. A place to crash. Help with university fees. Whatever."

"Well, in case you hadn't noticed, I'm an adult now. I don't need a father anymore."

"But it might have been nice to have one around when you were growing up, huh?"

Stephen cast his gaze down. "Whatever."

"For what it's worth, I wish I'd been able to be there for you from the beginning."

Stephen was silent for a long time before he said, "Why weren't you?"

The words and the hurt behind them made Patrick catch his breath. He thought back to all the times his father had been absent for him, but present for his half siblings. The last thing he wanted was for Stephen to have that same unwanted feeling.

"I didn't know you existed."

"Like hell you didn't."

Patrick glanced at Nadine and saw that she seemed puzzled, too. "Didn't your mother explain?"

"She said you were dead."

"What about in her letter?"

Silence.

Patrick muttered a curse. "I take it Zach never sent it to you. Did he tell you anything about our meeting?"

"Not much. He was pretty pissed about his hair. Said I owed him big-time."

That stupid dye job shouldn't have fooled him for a minute, Patrick realized now. "His hair will grow out. There are more important things at stake here."

"Like…?"

"Let me start at the beginning. About a month after your mother passed away, I came home from a trip to Alaska. In the mail I found a package with a return address from your apartment in Chelsea. Inside were two letters. One for me. One for you."

Stephen shifted forward, suddenly listening intently.

"In her letter, June told me that after we broke up she

found out she was pregnant. She said she decided not to tell me and to raise the child—you—on her own."

"That's not what she told me."

Patrick shrugged. "Why would she lie now? She left it up to me to decide whether to be a part of your life. But if I did decide to look you up, then she wanted me to give you a letter she'd written to you."

"And you gave it to Zach?"

Patrick nodded.

Stephen swore. "He called me after your meeting and didn't say a damn word about it."

"Have you seen Zach since then?" Nadine asked.

He shook his head.

"Maybe you should call him."

"You think I haven't tried? He hasn't returned any of my calls or text messages."

"Maybe because he didn't want you to know he was hitting your father up for money."

"What?" Stephen planted his hands on the table, his expression dumbfounded.

At least he hadn't been part of that plan, Patrick was relieved to find out. "He said something about needing money for a business. But I guess that won't be happening now."

"What a jerk."

Patrick couldn't agree more.

"Look, I apologize for that scam I pulled. But I still say all this is a waste of time. You say you're my father, and I guess that's the truth. But to me you're a stranger."

Was that really true? Did Stephen not feel any sort of connection between them? Patrick took a deep breath. He'd never thought this was going to be easy.

"Maybe if we got to know one another, it wouldn't feel so weird. Any chance you could get time off tomorrow and we could hit the hills?"

"No."

Well, that was pretty clear.

"Sorry, but this long-lost father routine is just...I don't know. Too little, too late."

Patrick felt at a loss as to what to try next. He'd already explained that he hadn't known he had a son. What else could he say?

At the very least, he needed to establish a route of communication. He dug out a business card from his wallet. "You may change your mind one day. Here's my phone number, address and e-mail."

Stephen shoved the card into his pocket without looking at it. In a jerky motion, he got up from his chair.

Patrick and Nadine stood, too.

"If you ever need a plane ticket back to New York, let me know. I've got an extra bedroom, if you'd like a place to hang in the city for a while."

"I've signed up to work until April."

"Your aunt says you're registered for college in the fall. I imagine the tuition's pretty steep."

"I'm planning on saving my money."

The kid was stubborn and independent, and Patrick felt oddly proud about that. "I'd be glad to help anyway."

Stephen shrugged. "I've got to get going. It was— interesting to meet you."

Patrick nodded. There were no words to describe this moment. His heart ached to the bursting point, yet he couldn't come up with any ideas to stop his son from walking back out of his life.

"ARE YOU OKAY?"

Patrick realized he was still standing, and sat down.

"That must have been so tough." Nadine's voice was tender.

"I can't believe I was fooled by Zach."

"That's easier to say once you've met the real Stephen."

"But even at the time I wondered why I didn't feel anything." He'd sure as hell felt something this time. God, he was *shaking*.

Nadine had noticed, too. She took his hand and held it between hers.

"June never should have written those letters," Patrick said.

"Why do you say that?"

"What was the point? Look at all the pain this has caused Stephen. He doesn't need this crap, especially not now when he's still in mourning for his mother."

"I think it's a good thing that he reacted so emotionally."

"Are you serious?"

"It shows that he has a big heart. That he cares. In the long run, that will play to your advantage. I honestly believe that one day Stephen will contact you. That he'll want you to be a part of his life."

Patrick's throat thickened with an unfamiliar emotion. He knew nothing about kids, only what he could remember from when he was that age. He'd been thrown into this too late and had nothing to offer Stephen, except what he'd promised.

He'd help with his education. He'd be someone to call in an emergency.

He hoped Stephen would eventually accept that. And it would be enough.

"I think we could use a few drinks over here." He signaled to the waiter. When he ordered Scotch, Nadine nodded. "Make that two."

"I've never seen you drink anything but wine or champagne."

"It's been a tough couple of days."

He couldn't argue with that. "Maybe they've been tougher than they needed to be."

"Oh?"

He'd been so angry at her before, but now all of that was gone. The roller-coaster journey of finding Stephen—he couldn't imagine having shared it with anyone else. When their drinks were served, he touched his glass to hers.

"Thank you for finding him. Not once, but twice. And being here. I guess I'm damn lucky Nathan wasn't in the day I showed up at your office."

"Why do you say Nathan, specifically? What if Lindsay had been available?"

"I only mentioned Nathan because of June's letter. She wrote that if I had trouble tracking down Stephen to call Nathan Fisher."

"Funny that she mentioned Nathan specifically."

"I suppose. Not that it matters, does it?"

"Probably not."

"I'm just glad it worked out the way it did. That's all I'm saying."

She looked at him solemnly. "Does this mean that you're not upset about my deception anymore?"

He nodded. It was true. The last of his resentment

toward her had slipped away, replaced by deeper, more profound emotions. He'd met his son for the first time today.

Hell. What else could matter in the face of that?

Patrick finished his drink, then raised his hand to order another. His head was still whirling from too much input, and not enough time to process.

Sort of like bungee jumping.

"We still haven't eaten," Nadine reminded him gently. "I think some food would be a good idea."

So they ordered an appetizer platter to share, as well as another round of Scotch. Nadine asked him about his Alaska book and as he talked about a subject that was both familiar and important to him, he gradually lost the free-falling sensation.

The food helped, too. At any rate, his hands were steady again.

"You okay to head up to our rooms now?"

With her comment he realized they were the only guests left in the lounge. Their waiter was chatting with the bartender, and the two of them looked pointedly in their direction.

He settled the bill, then they headed to their rooms. This time they were across the hall from one another. He unlocked Nadine's door for her, then passed her the key.

If memories crossed her mind from the night when they had meant to say good-night, but hadn't, she didn't give any sign.

Her expression as she looked at him was one of simple concern. "You going to be able to sleep?"

"I'm not sure," he answered honestly. Then, impulsively, he asked, "Want to watch a movie?"

She hesitated. "I'm not sure that's a good idea."

He couldn't blame her for her caution. Maybe if they'd moved more slowly from the beginning…but he couldn't bring himself to regret what had happened at Emerald Lake Lodge. The stuff that had happened later, yes. But not their night together.

He wanted her now as much as he had wanted her then. But even stronger than his desire, was his need to be close to her.

"Only a movie," he promised. "No ulterior motives. I need to give the emotions a chance to settle down."

That seemed to sway her. "Okay. Come on in, and we'll see what appeals."

Her room had a small seating area, with a sofa facing a cabinet that housed both a TV and a minibar. He picked up the remote control and read out movie titles, while she opened a bottle of water and poured two glasses.

She nixed a couple of his movie suggestions, then said yes to a comedy with Jim Carrey. Once the movie had started, she sat next to him, leaving a healthy foot of space between them.

The movie was enjoyable, with several good laughs, yet not for a second did Patrick lose his awareness of how close she was to him.

The urge to touch her was very strong. He wanted to cradle an arm around her, feel her head resting against his chest.

But he had made a promise that he intended to keep.

ALTHOUGH SHE WAS ENJOYING the story, Nadine dozed fitfully through the second half of the movie, the soundtrack proving as soothing as a lullaby. Then suddenly, there was no more talking, only music. Dimly she realized the movie was over and the credits were rolling.

The next thing she knew there was sudden silence and the room was very dark.

"Sorry. I should have turned on a lamp before I shut off the TV." Patrick groped in the dark for a few seconds before he located a lamp switch. An amber light pooled over his face.

He was smiling indulgently at her. "You didn't like the movie?"

"I did," she insisted. "I guess I was just tired."

Slowly Patrick's smile faded. His eyes seemed to grow bigger, his breathing louder. The room felt very small at that moment. The bed seemed very big.

She wanted to tell him that she wouldn't hold him to his promise. She wanted to kiss him. She wanted to be touched.

Most of all, she didn't want him to leave. Yet, she could see that he was about to move off the sofa. She touched his arm.

"Was June Stone the love of your life?"

His sucked in a breath. "Why do you ask that?"

It was something she'd longed to ask him for a long time now.

"I suppose I should say yes." He twisted his body and placed an arm along the sofa back, so he was facing her. "June was my first girlfriend. The first woman I made love to. And, as it turns out, the mother of my son."

"That's quite a list."

"No doubt she was an important woman in my life. But was she the *love* of my life? I'd have to say no."

"Well, then. Someone else?" She settled with her back against the sofa's arm, crossing her legs and resting her hands on her knees. It was a classic yoga pose, but she did not feel relaxed in the slightest.

"Always asking questions. Don't you think it should be my turn now? Who is the love of *your* life?"

She should have guessed he'd turn the tables and been prepared with an answer. But—there wasn't one. Thinking over the list of men she'd dated—most of them casually—no one stood out.

In fact, until she'd been with Patrick, she'd assumed she simply wasn't a very passionate person. He'd proved her wrong on that assumption, thankfully.

"I'm still waiting…"

She shrugged. "So am I."

He took a second to process that. "You mean, you haven't met him yet?"

"That's right," she said.

But that was a lie.

CHAPTER SEVENTEEN

PATRICK WAS JOLTED OUT of sleep as the plane rocked left, right, left, suddenly dropped elevation, then recovered.

Over the intercom, the pilot sounded unperturbed. "Folks, we've encountered a little turbulence. Please make sure your seat belts are fastened."

Patrick glanced at Nadine beside him. Her belt was properly in place, but she was gripping the magazine she'd bought at the Toronto airport as if she was afraid it was about to be ripped from her hands.

"You okay?"

She nodded tightly. "I've never been a fan of rough air."

He'd traveled enough to be inured to all but the most hair-raising of rides. He held out a hand and she accepted it with a grip that made him cringe.

"This is nothing. Want to hear about an experience I had on Iran Air once?"

"Oh—I don't think so."

He ran his thumb along the length of her fingers. She liked long dangling earrings, and he'd seen her wear bracelets and necklaces. But she never wore rings.

He wondered what it would be like to be the man to give her a diamond. To slide the ring over her slender finger, then to look into her eyes and to know that she would be his....

The plane jostled again, and her fingers crunched his hand. He winced and tried to think of something to distract her.

"Give me another one of those questions," he said. "You know, the Proust game."

"Um, okay…" She took a deep breath, thought for a bit, then asked, "What is the quality you admire most in a woman?"

Once upon a time he might have answered courage, or adventurousness, honesty or strength. But his understanding of himself and what he appreciated had changed since he'd met Nadine and he struggled to put a word on that one, most beguiling characteristic.

And then he saw her tuck her hair behind her ear with her free hand, and he knew.

"Grace." That one word went beyond her movements to encompass the essence of her personality. The way she treated strangers and tackled her work…and made love.

Ever since they'd left Kicking Horse Resort this morning, he'd been trying to convince himself that this would be their last day together, that when the cab dropped her home tonight, he would be waving farewell for good.

But all the while he'd known that he was fooling himself. He wanted her in his life. He had to find a way to make it happen.

BY THE LAST LEG OF THEIR journey, Nadine was exhausted. When Patrick gave the cab driver her address, she didn't have the strength to object. Her eyes burned and her head ached, but she couldn't doze off now any more than she had been able to do on the two flights they'd taken today.

It wasn't just the turbulence that had kept her awake.

There was so much unsaid between her and Patrick and it was driving her crazy. She knew he was as attracted to her as she was to him. At the same time, she guessed he had the same doubts about starting a relationship as she did. After all, they had very little in common.

But maybe it was those differences that were the big attraction.

Patrick waved away the doorman and carried her bag up the stairs, stopping outside the vestibule to say farewell. It was very late, past midnight, and her ears still felt blocked from the change in air pressure. She put her hands on his arms to steady herself. Even through the thickness of his jacket, she could feel the unyielding hardness of his muscles.

"I guess this is goodbye," she said. The city was uncharacteristically quiet. She could hear his breath drawing in, then out. The streetlights were bright enough that she could see signs of struggle in his expression.

"Maybe it should be goodbye. But that's not what I want."

She almost laughed with relief. "Me, either."

She let her head sink to his chest. His arms engulfed her, holding her close as if he couldn't stand to let go.

"When can I see you again?"

Dinner out, or a movie. Both would be safe choices. But Nadine thought they were already beyond safe choices. She tipped her head up so she could see his eyes. "Would you like to come to dinner at my parents' next Sunday?"

He swallowed. She could almost feel his panic. But before she could doubt the sincerity of his intentions, he nodded.

"Dinner on Sunday would be wonderful."

It wouldn't be. Her parents would make the situation uncomfortable and awkward. Yet, in her heart, she felt this was what she needed to do. She had no idea where her relationship with Patrick was headed, but he was important to her.

And she knew she was tired of secrets, and half-truths and never feeling free to be completely herself.

Patrick placed his warm hands on either side of her face. He kissed her gently, once, then pulled back to gaze at her.

"Your parents are going to love me."

His bravado made her smile. The look in his eyes filled her with warmth. This was a moment she wanted to stamp into her heart forever—

"Hey, you two. Remember me?"

Nadine started and glanced back at the street. The cab driver had rolled down the passenger's side window so he could call out to them. She supposed it was more considerate than honking his horn.

PATRICK SPENT THE NEXT few days preparing for his book tour, and steeling himself for the occasion of meeting Nadine's parents. She'd let him take her out for lunch once, but other than that, they hadn't seen one another since their trip to Kicking Horse.

He sensed this was some sort of test. That having rushed into bed together so quickly after they'd met, Nadine was now pulling back, wanting him to prove that he wasn't just interested in the sexual side of their relationship.

Well, he had no problem with that. It was a test that

he would pass with flying colors, because right from the beginning he'd known Nadine was something special.

On Sunday evening, he had a cab drop him off at Nadine's apartment. They'd agreed to walk from there to her parents' home eight blocks away.

Christmas lights sparkled against the fresh fallen snow, and Patrick thought he'd never seen the city looking so pretty. Nor Nadine.

She looked lovely enough to be the angel on top of a tree, with her hair curled in waves around her face and her cheeks cherry-pink from the cold.

When she stopped in front of a five-story mansion, his mood dampened. "This is it?"

She nodded.

Having recently purchased his own co-op apartment, Patrick knew real estate prices in Manhattan very well. This place, he guessed, would sell for around thirty to forty million dollars.

He'd realized Nadine's family was wealthy. They owned Waverly Hotels, for God's sake. But this kind of money was insane.

"You aren't going to back out now, are you?"

"Of course not." But he wanted to. God, how he wanted to.

"Okay. Let's do this."

She'd looked so pretty and carefree as they were walking, but now as they entered her parents' house, he could sense her trepidation, almost as strongly as his own.

For a moment he was awed by the splendor of the foyer—with its vaulted ceiling, marble floor and an enormous oil painting placed for maximum impact as you stepped inside.

A woman in a demure black dress, who looked about the right age to be Nadine's grandmother, bustled toward them.

"Martha." Nadine hugged her warmly. "This is Patrick O'Neil. Martha runs this place," she explained to him, and as he met the woman's steely gaze, he realized that her approval was probably as important as Nadine's parents'.

He was glad he'd worn a shirt and jacket as he slipped off his winter coat. Martha immediately whisked it from his hands.

"Go ahead, honey," she told Nadine. "Your parents are already in the music hall."

Patrick had never been in a grander home. Mutely he followed as Nadine led him into a large room containing a huge fireplace with a stone mantel, the kind of uncomfortable-looking furniture you saw in antique shops and a magnificent grand piano.

The setting only occupied his senses for a few seconds, before the people in the room drew his attention. A tall, portly man in suit and tie, and a lovely, petite woman with styled hair, pearls and a smile just like her daughter's, only frosty and tight.

Patrick took a deep breath and smiled. People were people, right? And he'd never had trouble getting along with anyone in his life.

After introductions, he was offered a drink and then began a series of questions which turned out to be a polite version of a police inquisition. Where had he grown up? Where did he go to school? Who was his mother, and his father? What about his grandparents?

Finally Nadine interrupted. "You should be asking about Patrick's travels. He has so many amazing stories."

Her approving smile was as fortifying as the excellent Scotch in his glass. After a long swallow, he decided to launch into one of his no-fail stories.

"The funny thing about balloons is you never have one hundred percent control over where the darn thing is going to land…"

He'd told this story in school gymnasiums and church basements, at book signing events and fundraisers, for children and adult audiences alike.

Without exception, *everyone* liked the ballooning story where, defying careful calculations, unexpected winds had him landing the balloon and his three passengers, in the midst of an outdoor wedding, at just the moment the bride and groom were about to say their vows.

"That must have been very distressing for the family," was Sophia's only comment.

"You do a lot of hot-air ballooning, do you?" asked Wilfred, pushing his glasses higher on his nose and frowning.

"That was two years ago. I was researching a book on New Mexico. Albuquerque hosts an amazing hot-air balloon fiesta every October and I figured the best way to experience that was in the air, rather than from the ground."

"Tell me, Patrick. Have you ever had a real job?"

Patrick polished off his Scotch. "Define *real*."

"Something that involves work. Not flying balloons and climbing mountains and all that nonsense."

Patrick glanced at Nadine. She was literally on the edge of her seat, her eyes begging him to…do what? How did she expect him to react to her father's rudeness?

He turned back to the older man and shrugged. "I earn a very good living with my books."

"Money isn't everything," Wilfred said.

But Patrick suspected that money actually *was* everything, at least in this household. But it had to be a *lot* of money. And preferably some of it had to have been passed down by your ancestors.

He was relieved when Martha returned to announce that dinner was served. This involved going up a massive circular staircase to the next floor, which housed a dining room large enough to accommodate twenty guests or more.

The table had been made up for their smaller party, though. And as Patrick took his spot, he vowed to let his hosts do the talking for a while.

He wondered how the Waverlys would respond to the Proust Questionnaire, but as if she could sense that he had mischief up his sleeve, Nadine quickly took control of the conversation.

During the three courses of soup, salad and rack of lamb, she steered the conversation between topics that were obviously her parents' favorites.

With the focus off him, Patrick began to appreciate that both her parents were quite intelligent and actually did possess a sense of humor.

But then Martha appeared again, this time to announce that coffee and dessert was ready in the library. Patrick was glad to have Nadine by his side for a bit. He placed a hand on the small of her back and leaned forward to whisper in her ear.

"Another room? More food? I can't believe this."

She jabbed him with her elbow. "Shh. I warned you about the usual routine."

"They really eat this way every single evening?"

"Shh," she said again as they entered the most amazing library he'd ever seen. Bookshelves lined all of the walls, even above and below the windows. In the center of the room were leather chairs surrounding a marble table, upon which was a silver coffee service, bowls of crème brûlée and a tray of cheese and dried fruit.

It was hard to take in. How did they manage? Didn't they ever want to put up their feet, order in pizza and watch a movie?

Patrick was hoping to remain out of the limelight for this final course, but unfortunately for him, Sophia Waverly decided that it was her turn to direct the conversation.

"So, Patrick, tell me how you met my daughter."

Oh, Lord. He saw panic in Nadine's eyes and decided that brevity was the key here. "I met her when I retained the services of The Fox & Fisher Detective Agency."

"I thought you met at that rain forest gala?" her father asked.

Oops. He glanced at Nadine, realizing they should have gotten their stories straight. "That was later on the same day," he said.

"Was your case the reason Nadine had to fly to Canada twice this month?" Sophia asked.

"That's right."

Sophie seemed to be waiting for him to say more. He cleared his throat. "She was helping me find my son."

"He'd gone missing? How old is he?"

"Stephen is eighteen. And he hadn't gone missing. I'd just found out that he existed. And I wanted to meet him."

Sophia pulled back in amazement and shock. She glanced from him, to her husband, then to her daughter. "How is this possible?"

Patrick wanted to show Nadine's parents the utmost respect. But these were details he simply wasn't going to share. "It's a long story," he said. "I wouldn't want to bore you."

The Waverlys refrained from inquiring further. But he could see they were judging him on the facts that they did know—and finding him irresponsible and promiscuous at best, amoral at worst.

Nadine glanced at her watch. "I didn't realize it was so late. I'm afraid we have to run. Patrick is leaving for a five-week book tour tomorrow."

"Well, then I suppose he had better be on his way," Wilfred said. "But there's no reason you need to leave so early, honey."

Patrick waited, almost expecting Nadine to give in to the obvious wishes of her parents. But she just laughed.

"Don't be silly, Dad. Of course I have to run, as well. I'll see you both on Wednesday. Don't have Martha see us out. I have my key. I'll make sure to lock up."

"I'M SORRY, I'M SORRY, I'm sorry!" Nadine kissed him once for each apology she gave him. "They were dreadful. I'm so sorry."

Patrick accepted her kisses willingly enough, but she could see that it would take more than a few words and smooches to make this up to him.

"Well, at least now I understand why you didn't want to work for the family business," he said, as they began to walk in the direction of her apartment.

His comment stung, even though it was true. Her parents drove her crazy, but she still loved them and it hurt to know that Patrick couldn't see beyond their faults.

But then again, why should he?

For me. He should do it for me....

She blanked out the little voice inside of her. There would be other dinners. Lots of time for them to adjust to one another. She would talk to her parents. Make them understand that next time they had better be on their best behavior.

At her apartment door, she went willingly into Patrick's arms. When he kissed her, she felt a delicious heat that blocked out the winter wind. "I can't believe you're going to be gone for five weeks."

"I'll be home three days for Christmas. But you're right. It's going to feel damn long." He put a hand to her cheek. His fingers felt ice-cold. She wrapped her hand around his palm and brought it to her lips for a kiss.

"You're chilled. I'd feel really guilty if you got sick right before your tour."

He arched his eyebrows. "I'm touched by your concern."

"Would you like to come in and warm up?

"Sweetheart, I thought you'd never ask. Though parts of me are already pretty hot."

AFTER THE MAGNIFICENCE of Nadine's parents' mansion, Patrick was almost afraid to see the inside of her two-bedroom apartment. But he was pleasantly surprised to find her home comfortable and unpretentious.

He was willing to concede that the furnishings and artwork were probably way more expensive than they looked. But at least they didn't shout "Money" and "Don't Touch" the way her parents' belongings did.

"Do you want anything to drink?" Nadine asked.

He removed her coat and placed it on a bench covered in a fuzzy ivory fabric. "I want nothing but you."

He pulled her body close and watched as her eyelashes fanned her cheeks. Then they swept up and she had him captured with her eyes.

"Music?" she asked.

"If you like." He didn't need anything to set the mood. Just being alone with her was enough.

But she turned a knob on a panel next to the light switch, and suddenly there was soft piano music and a woman's husky voice in the room with them.

As he kissed her, he tried not to think that this would be their last night together for three weeks, or that he despised her parents or that his son didn't seem interested in getting to know him.

This wasn't a night to dwell on any of those problems.

She swayed to the music as she kissed him, her mouth and tongue moving in concert with the beat. God, he'd been afraid that his memories had been overblown, but she was every bit as warm and passionate as he remembered.

Gently, he ran his hands down the length of her back until he had her derriere in his hands. He guided the movement of her body, blending her rhythm into his, melding their bodies as much as their clothing would allow.

"I could—change into something more comfortable," she suggested, her mouth against his ear.

He'd been thinking of getting her out of her clothes entirely. The sooner, the better. But he didn't have to leave for the airport until nine the next morning, and his suitcase was already packed.

"Go ahead," he told her, releasing her with reluctance. "But don't be long. We have ten hours and I don't want to waste a minute."

CHAPTER EIGHTEEN

FOR THE FIRST TIME SINCE SHE'D started as the receptionist, Nadine was late for work on Monday. She hadn't been able to tear herself away from her apartment until Patrick had left for his plane. Since she'd hardly slept all night, she knew she looked terrible. But today, for once, she didn't care.

Last night had been amazing. Not just the lovemaking, which had been scream-out-loud fantastic for both of them, but the cuddling after, the bathing together, the snacking in the kitchen, then back to bed to fall asleep, only to wake again to the feel of Patrick's hand on her bare bottom, sliding down her thigh, then gradually up, his fingers gliding over her softest flesh, between hot, damp folds...

"You're twenty minutes late, you know." Tamara Maynard was behind the receptionist's desk. She was typing up a report.

"I know." Nadine could feel her cheeks growing hot. "Did I miss anything?"

"Just a potential client. Lindsay's talking to her in the conference room."

Oh, darn.

"Of course, if you're not busy, you could always walk me through the filing system again."

Nadine narrowed her eyes. Was she being made fun of? Before she could decide, Nathan emerged from his office. "Hey, there you are. Mrs. Waldgrave is coming in for an update this morning. Do you have the report ready?"

"I do." Last week when she'd dropped off the evidence at the local precinct, she'd been assured that the Flower Con Man would soon be behind bars and would stay there.

"Great." He handed her the file. "You take care of that and I'll work on paying a few bills around here." He was about to step back into his office, when he gave her a second glance. "You look different."

"She got laid last night is my bet."

"Tamara!" Nadine wheeled on her, just as Lindsay and her client were exiting the conference room. Everyone fell silent as Lindsay walked the elderly man to the door. As soon as he was gone, Lindsay whirled around.

"Nadine. Is it true? Are you hot and heavy with Patrick O'Neil?"

"Really?" Nathan rubbed his head. "You're dating Patrick O'Neil? Why wasn't I told?"

"Oh, keep up, Nathan. I did tell you."

"Stop it already." Nadine couldn't believe how childishly they were behaving. "This isn't junior high and my love life—"

She stopped suddenly, realizing that she didn't feel at all angry. In fact, she'd never been happier in her life. And these people weren't just colleagues. They were her friends—well, except for Tamara.

"My love life is absolutely wonderful. And that's all I have to say about it. Except that he's just left for the first three weeks of his book tour and I'm going to miss him so much."

"Will he be back for Christmas?" Lindsay asked. "And New Year's Eve? Of course you'll bring him to the wedding."

"He isn't back in the city until the twenty-fourth. They actually have a book signing set up on Christmas Eve from seven to nine. Then he's all mine for two-and-a-half days. I'm afraid your wedding is out, though. He leaves on the twenty-seventh for the last two weeks of his tour."

"He won't be around much, then. But don't worry. We'll keep you so busy, you'll hardly miss him," Lindsay promised.

The phone rang and as Tamara answered the call, Lindsay took Nadine by the arm and headed for her office. "I'll give you your pick of jobs. We have—"

"Everyone, news flash." Tamara had just hung up the phone and she waited until all of them were paying attention. "Kate's husband just called. They're at the hospital. She's going to have the baby any second."

THAT EVENING, NADINE LEFT a message on Patrick's phone and also sent him an e-mail. She had his book-tour schedule on her fridge so she knew he was in Boston. His book reading and signing event was scheduled to end at nine, yet by ten-thirty he still hadn't returned her call.

She tried his number again at eleven, then eleven-thirty. Finally she reached him.

"Nadine. Sorry, I had my phone off. Is anything wrong?"

She'd been so excited to tell him the news earlier. Now she tried to muster the same enthusiasm. "Kate had her baby today!"

"Really? Boy or girl?"

He didn't sound very thrilled…but then, he didn't know Kate or Jay. Still, she just had to share the news.

"A baby girl, six pounds, ten ounces. Lindsay, Nathan and I went for a short visit. Kate is such a trouper, she was already out of bed, changing the baby's diaper and dressing her in these cute little sleepers."

"I'm glad everyone's healthy."

Nadine curled up on the sofa and pulled a blanket over her legs. She wished she could find the words to share how magical the day had been. Kate had showed her how to rest the baby against her chest, with her tiny head turned to one side.

"Kate let me hold her. We haven't had any babies in our family for years. I'd forgotten how lovely they are, and how soft and warm."

"I've never held a baby," Patrick said. "I don't think I'd know how."

He had missed all of this with his own son. Nadine knew it had to hurt. Whatever had June been thinking to cut him out of the picture so completely?

At the hospital Nathan had put his arms around Lindsay when it was her turn to hold the baby, and Jay had been so sweet to Kate. Nadine had found her thoughts turning to something she'd never considered much before…

Marriage, children, family.

Of course, it was much too soon to think about these things with Patrick.

Still, she had missed him.

"I wish you'd been here," she said softly.

"Me, too. But at least the reading went well. I was

surprised how many people showed up and they almost all bought at least one copy of the book."

"Congratulations. Is that why you were late getting back to your room? Did your signing run overtime?"

"No. The store was closing, so we had to leave promptly at nine. I went out with a couple of the organizers for drinks and a late dinner. That's why I didn't get your message until now."

She felt a pang of jealousy that he'd been out with people she didn't even know. Were they guys? Or women?

She didn't ask. She couldn't ask. She had to trust him, and of course, she did.

"I should get some sleep, sweetheart. Tomorrow starts early with a spot on an early-morning talk show, followed by two more signings."

"That sounds so glamorous."

"Trust me, it's not. I'd far rather be with you."

If she was a cat, she would have purred. "In twenty days you will be. Not that I'm counting."

"I like the idea of you counting. I will be, too. Last night was pretty amazing, Nadine. The timing of this damn tour couldn't have been worse."

"At least you'll be home for Christmas."

"Yeah. I've been wondering what to do about that for Stephen. I left it up to him whether he wants to get in touch with me or not. But do you think it would be okay if I sent him a Christmas present?"

"Definitely. That's an excellent idea." A few olive branches couldn't hurt.

"Talk to you tomorrow, sweetheart. Sleep tight."

Nadine kept holding on to the phone, even after the connection to Patrick had ended. She hadn't been ready for their conversation to end. There was so much she felt like talking to him about.

Like babies.

Did he even want children one day?

There was still a lot she didn't know about this man she was falling in love with.

THE NEXT TIME SHE HAD DINNER with her parents, Nadine was determined to discuss their treatment of Patrick. She was planning to wait until they introduced the subject, but they'd gone through cocktails and the main course without breathing a word about him.

They asked her questions about her job and about Kate's baby. They discussed music, city politics and a play her parents had seen that week.

When it came time for dessert in the library, Nadine had to wonder if they had possibly forgotten about him.

"We should have lunch this Friday," her mother suggested, "to go over the Christmas schedule."

There were always numerous parties to attend during the holiday season. This was nothing new, and Nadine tried to get to as many as possible, since it made her mother very happy.

"Okay, Mom. We can do lunch."

"Then there are the usual family celebrations, which I'm sure I don't need to remind you of. Christmas Eve at Aunt Eileen's—"

"Sorry, but I won't be able to make Christmas Eve dinner this year." Traditionally this was when she saw all her cousins, aunts, uncles and grandparents. There were so many, she doubted her absence would matter. "Patrick gets back from his book tour that day. He's doing one last signing at Strand, which I'm going to attend. And then we're spending the rest of the evening together."

Silence greeted that announcement. Her father added sugar to his coffee. Her mother reached for a dish of brandy-soaked berries drizzled with white chocolate.

Nadine had expected at least a token argument since this would be the first year she wouldn't spend the night with them, sleeping in her old bedroom.

"Christmas dinner will be here, of course," her mother continued, as if Nadine hadn't said anything. "Just a small family affair as usual."

"I assume Patrick will be welcome?"

Her mother sighed deeply. "So that's still on then."

"Of course it's still on. I brought him here to meet you just one week ago."

Again, no one said anything, and now she really began to feel angry. "The way you two behaved that night…it was embarrassing. You've never treated a friend of mine like that before."

"In the past you displayed good taste in friends."

Her friends had all been met at schools her parents had selected, parties and galas she attended for their sake. For the first time, Nadine realized how much her parents had controlled her life before she started her job at Fox & Fisher. Was that the real reason they'd objected so strenuously to her decision to work in the private investigation field?

Not because the work was potentially dangerous, but because she would be meeting all sorts of people, going to all sorts of places, and they would have no say over any of it.

She knew part of the reason they were protective

was because of Liz. But she was so different from her cousin, there really was no reason for them to worry.

"I don't see why you would object to Patrick. Mom, your committee booked him as a speaker, for heaven's sake. You must agree he's an intelligent, well-spoken man, who has done a lot of interesting things with his life."

"He's a traveler," her father said, his voice gruff. "An adventurer. Not the right sort of man for our daughter."

"But that isn't your call. I'm twenty-seven. Old enough to know when I'm falling in love."

Her parents both shook their heads. "What you feel for him isn't love, dear," her mother said.

"Certainly we can see why this man might appeal to you," her father added. "But it isn't the sort of relationship you should allow to become serious."

"I can't believe you're actually speaking to me like this." She put down her coffee cup and saucer. "I came here tonight determined to tell you both that your behavior the other night wasn't acceptable. And you have the nerve to give *me* a lecture?"

"Nadine." Her father threw his napkin on the table, while her mother covered her mouth with her hand.

She'd shocked them both, and she'd actually shocked herself, as well. She'd never spoken to either of them this way before. Because, until now, nothing had seemed important enough to cause a row about. Still, she'd always assumed that they valued her opinion. That they trusted her.

"I'm serious, Mom. Dad. If Patrick isn't welcome here for Christmas dinner, then I won't be showing up, either."

"You can't possibly mean that," her mother said.

She could tell her mother was on the verge of tears. And she hated that. But in her heart she knew she had to take this stand.

"I do mean it. Not only do I expect you to invite Patrick to Christmas dinner, but I expect you to treat him with the same degree of respect and consideration that you treat all your guests."

Her parents looked as if she'd punched them.

She left the room because there was nothing more to say. Martha tried to talk to her as she was leaving... "What happened? Are you all right?" But she waved her off. She couldn't speak. Not yet. She couldn't even think—it was as if her brain had grown numb.

It was only when she was out on the street, heading for home, that the significance of what had happened sank in. She'd basically estranged herself from her family.

She kept her chin up as the tears pooled in her eyes.

PATRICK CALLED HER LATE that night. "So where were you? I've been trying to reach you for hours."

"Oh...dinner at my parents'." She waited to see if he would ask for details about the evening, but he didn't. He had several stories about his day that he was excited to share.

She listened, deciding that it was best this way. She didn't think she could describe the conversation between her and her parents without crying. Besides she didn't want him to worry about her.

When it came time to say good-night, Patrick said, "Soon I'll be holding you in my arms again, sweetheart."

"I wish I didn't have to wait."

"Only fourteen more days."

As the holidays drew closer, business at the agency was slowing down. Nadine didn't think they'd had a new client all week, which was just as well. No one had their mind focused on work right now.

Lindsay and Nathan were handling last-minute details for their New Year's Eve wedding, Tamara was taking longer and longer lunches as she worked on her Christmas shopping list, and Nadine was using every excuse she could find to spend time with Kate and her baby.

The baby had been named Alice, and she was getting cuter and more responsive with every day. Since Nadine was supposed to be cleaning up the tail end of Kate's cases, she could usually come up with a couple of legitimate reasons to visit every week.

On the final Monday before Christmas, she had some billings that needed Kate's okay. She popped into Nathan's office, where he was busy on the computer conducting background checks.

She showed him the stack of billings. "You wanted these in the mail before we break for the holidays, but they're Kate's clients, so I was going to have her look them over."

"Let me guess. You're going in person and you'll look after Alice while she's working." Nathan grinned. Everyone in the office loved the baby, but Nadine was the one who had gone completely gaga over her.

"That's the plan." Nadine didn't bother trying to deny her ulterior motive.

"Go ahead. If anything pops up, I'll handle it. I'm going to be in the office all afternoon anyway."

As she passed by Tamara's desk, she noticed the receptionist was affixing labels onto her personal greeting cards. Tamara noticed her staring and shrugged. "Hey, I don't have anything else to do."

When Nadine had been receptionist, she had always been able to find something to do during lulls in business, but she didn't point this out.

The day of reckoning was approaching for Tamara... she'd been working here three weeks. When the trial period was over, Nadine would have more than a few observations to bring up with Lindsay and Nathan.

Nadine took the subway to Kate and Jay's place, which now looked more like a day care than a sophisticated New York City apartment. Kate met her at the door, with Alice in her arms.

"Eric's out of school for the holidays, so he and Jay have gone to the gym to shoot baskets. Jay's trying to spend extra time with him, so he doesn't end up resenting this little one." Kate touched her nose to the baby's. "Because Alice really is an attention-hog."

"No kidding." Nadine dropped the papers on Kate's kitchen counter and went to hold the baby. "She is some major cute. And how about you? Are you getting much sleep?"

"Honestly, no. But she is so worth it." Kate's red hair was in a bun and she was wearing an outfit that straddled the line between sweat suit and pajamas, but the happiness on her face made her truly beautiful.

She grabbed the handful of invoices. "I take it these need my approval?"

"Yes, please." Nadine cuddled Alice close, then noticed a sour smell. "Does she need her diaper changed?"

"I just fed her, so probably. Here, hand her back—"

"I'll do it." Kate had a temporary changing station set

up in the corner of the living room, and Nadine took the baby there.

"Hmm." Kate shuffled through the papers. "These all look fine. You're doing a great job handling my cases, Nadine. Are you enjoying the work?"

"I sure am."

"And what about Patrick? Is he going to be home soon?"

"On Christmas Eve. I can't wait."

"Yeah? Then what's bothering you? Last week you looked like you were walking on air. Today, I hate to say it, but you seem depressed."

Nadine hadn't intended to tell Kate her problems. But as she unsnapped the baby's sleeper, the story came gushing out of her. "I had a big confrontation with my parents the other night. For some reason they don't approve of Patrick. I told them if he wasn't welcome in their home, then I wouldn't be coming for Christmas dinner, either. I keep expecting them to phone and tell me they've changed their minds. But it's been over a week and I haven't heard a word."

Kate couldn't possibly understand how unusual that was. Nadine usually had at least one call a day from her mother. Now—nothing.

"Oh, dear. Are you sorry you gave them that ultimatum?"

"I didn't have a choice. But I never thought they would be this rigid." Nadine cleaned Alice's bottom, then positioned a fresh diaper under her.

When the job was done, Nadine washed her hands, then held Alice close to her chest, in her favorite position. For once Alice didn't fall asleep. Her big blue eyes gazed up at Nadine. "She's focusing better now," Nadine noticed.

"It's amazing how quickly she changes," Kate agreed. "Hard to believe that one day she and I might be arguing about her boyfriends, too."

FINALLY IT WAS CHRISTMAS EVE. As she watched Patrick sign books and talk to his fans, knowing that in just a few hours she would have him all to herself, Nadine thought she was close to perfect happiness.

The only stain on this nearly flawless day was the fact that she still hadn't heard a word from her parents. She couldn't believe that they would rather she didn't come to Christmas dinner at all, than come with Patrick.

She pulled out her cell phone and checked the display. No missed calls. No messages.

Apparently they were holding firm to their ridiculous position. Well, so be it.

She smiled as she noticed Patrick heading toward her. Behind him the store employees were tidying up after the signing and putting away the few copies of the book that hadn't sold.

"Sweetheart. Finally." He pulled her into his arms and kissed her. "It's over. We can go home now."

Before he'd started the book signing, he'd read snippets from various sections while a video had played in the background, showing him scuba diving and surfing and hang gliding. In all the footage, his body was amazingly tanned and fit, and he made whatever he was doing look easy and effortless.

Nadine had noticed the looks the women in the crowd

gave him. She realized that Patrick had been attracting this sort of attention in every city on his tour.

And yet, he had come home to her.

He wanted *her*.

She clung to his arm as they headed outside to find a cab. It was a cold, clear night and she had stocked her apartment with everything they would need for at least three days.

That was how long he had, until he had to leave to complete the publicity tour.

"I can't wait to get you all to myself," he said, once they were cuddled in the backseat of a cab. He cupped her face and kissed the tip of her nose. "Thank you for being so patient."

She was still blown away by how many people had come out to hear him, to meet him, to buy one of his books. "Until tonight I didn't realize how much of a celebrity you are."

"Hardly a celebrity. But I must admit I've sold a lot of books the past three weeks. I think even your parents might be impressed. I assume we'll be seeing them tomorrow?"

Outside, the Christmas lights were passing in a blur as the cab emerged from the heavy Midtown traffic and picked up speed. "No. We have the whole three days all to ourselves."

"I love the sound of that. But surely we need to spend some time with your family. For Christmas dinner, at least."

She shook her head. During a few of their phone conversations, Patrick had raised the subject of seeing her parents over the holidays. Each time she'd managed to divert him onto a different topic.

She'd hoped that in time, she'd be able to discuss this without crying. But the subject was still too painful.

"What's going on? Why won't you look at me?"

"W-we had a falling out."

"You mean, you and your mom and dad?"

She nodded.

"But—" Suddenly he understood. "Because of me?"

She nodded again.

"Oh, hell. Sweetheart, I'm sorry. Tell me what happened."

In a faltering voice she relayed the essence of their conversation. And resolutely she insisted that she wasn't sorry she'd said what she'd said.

"I hadn't realized how much I'd let them control my life. Working at Fox & Fisher was really the first time I defied them. I thought they were finally coming round to the idea that I was an adult and responsible for making my own decisions. But obviously not."

"I hate being the cause of this rift."

"It's not your fault. I should have stood up to them years ago. I just—I always wanted to please them. Their approval meant so much to me. Too much."

The cab stopped in front of her building. Patrick clasped her shoulder. "We'll talk about this later. Right now, we have some catching up to do."

CHAPTER NINETEEN

IT WAS CRAZY HOW MUCH HE'D missed her, Patrick thought. He'd never imagined he would feel this way about a woman. Want her so much. *Love* her so much.

He'd always been a man of passion, but those passions had been for other things. For travel and adventure and living on the edge.

Women had always been in the picture, but on the periphery, when it was convenient.

"Three weeks is much too long to go without *you*." He carried her over the threshold and took her directly to the bedroom. "I hope you don't have any plans for the next three hours."

"I promised you the next three days," she reminded him, her fingers on the top button of her blouse.

He watched as she slowly unfastened the row of buttons. With teasing slowness, she drew the fabric from her shoulders, revealing a red satin bra, her perfect ivory cleavage.

"My turn." He took a moment to enjoy the view. Her dark hair had fallen over one shoulder, the curls just reached the top of her breast. Though she wasn't airbrushed perfection, she was more beautiful to him than any cover model ever could be.

He ran his hands over the satin material, felt her breasts budding under his touch. Then he reached around her to unfasten the bra and slip it off her body.

He continued unwrapping her in this way, like a treasured Christmas present, and at the end he shucked his own clothing and drew her to him.

"I need you inside me. Now."

He felt her shudder in his arms, heard her sigh, then gasp, then cry.

Too long. It had been too long. He tangled his fist around her hair and tasted the skin at her neck, her throat, her breast.

It was happening too quickly, but he couldn't make himself slow down. She was too perfect. Everything, everything, everything he wanted.

Was with her.

THERE WASN'T MUCH SLEEP that night, only a few hours. When Nadine opened her eyes and saw that light was slipping through the cracks in the blinds, she couldn't believe it.

"Merry Christmas, sweetheart." She kissed the back of Patrick's neck, but he didn't budge.

At home—at her parents' home—breakfast would be served casually, by the enormous twenty-foot Christmas tree in the living room. Hanging from the oak mantel would be three beautifully embroidered stockings—only two this year. It had been a childish tradition, she supposed, but she felt sad that this year marked the end of it.

She rolled onto her stomach and noticed a strange movement amid Patrick's discarded clothing on the floor. She stretched out an arm to investigate and found his cell phone, set on Vibrate.

"You have a call," she said. "Do you want to answer it?"

He moaned and rolled onto his back.

She glanced at the display. The name was familiar, and then it hit her. "It's from Diane Stone."

"What?" Patrick lifted his head. "June's sister?"

"Yes." She passed him the phone and he quickly turned it on.

"Patrick here." He listened for a minute, his eyes growing wider. "Yes. I see."

More waiting on her part. Then Patrick spoke again. "Of course you can."

He sat up, brushed the hair back from his forehead. "I have to go out of town on the twenty-seventh. Any chance you could make it tomorrow?"

He was making plans for one of the few precious days he'd promised to her. Nadine clutched the bedding to her chest as he ended the call. For a few moments he stared at the phone disbelievingly, then gave her a rueful smile.

"That was Stephen."

"Really?" She couldn't believe it, either. "How wonderful that he called. But his aunt's name was on call display. Isn't Stephen still in Canada?"

"You know how I wanted to send him something for Christmas? Well, I gave him an air voucher. Turned out they'd had no snow for the past three weeks. He was able to shuffle his work schedule around so he could get a week off. Last night he flew to his aunt's. And he wants to see me tomorrow."

IT WAS THE MOST UNIQUE Christmas Day Nadine had ever spent, and also the most romantic. Patrick had bought her one memento from every city on his book tour, and he had a cute story to match, explaining how each item—from a bottle of Cashmere Mist perfume, to a huge assortment of Ghirardelli chocolates—had reminded him of her.

They drank champagne and orange juice while they soaked in the tub, then later they feasted on roast turkey breast, cranberry chutney and vegetables from the cooked-food counter at Dean & DeLuca, while they watched *Miracle on 34th Street* at her pleading.

As the sun began to set on the day, they decided to go for a walk in Central Park. She hoped the fresh air and exercise would take her mind away from what she was missing—a six-course Christmas dinner with her mom and dad.

She supposed Patrick would have found the event dreadfully dull, but she had always loved the tradition, and Christmas was the one holiday when she actually enjoyed putting on a pretty dress and making a fuss.

A gust of wind whipped her hair and sent her scarf flying as they rounded a corner. Patrick caught the end and twisted it back around her neck.

"I wonder what made Stephen decide to visit now?"

"He said he'd finally managed to get that letter from Zach. Maybe something June wrote made him willing to give me a second chance."

She squeezed his hand. "It's really your first chance. I hope he understands that."

"And I hope you don't mind that we aren't going to

be able to spend tomorrow together. I promised you three days. It's ending up to be more like one and a half."

She ignored the empty feeling in the pit of her stomach at the thought of him leaving again. "That's okay. Spending time with Stephen is important. Anyway, you only have two more weeks until the book tour ends."

"True enough."

"Though I was wondering about New Year's Eve... Is there any chance you could fly back to New York for Lindsay and Nathan's wedding?"

It would mean a lot to her if he could come, she almost added, but she didn't because a frown was forming on his face.

She waited, preparing herself for disappointment.

"I don't think it's possible to get back early, sweetheart. I'm sorry. My plan was to fly you to Los Angeles for New Year's."

"I can't. The wedding."

"Right. Well, we will have some time together after the book tour. At least a few weeks."

She stopped walking. "Only a few weeks? And then what?"

"I'll be off to Canada to work on the next book. I did tell you I'd signed another contract, right?"

"Yes. But I didn't realize you'd be starting it so quickly. Don't you ever take some time off between projects?"

"Like I said, I'll take a few weeks. Maybe a month this time," he added with a smile.

A month. She kicked at a sad pile of leaves left over from the fall. "How much time do you usually spend in the city? On average?"

"In the past, one or two months a year."

His apartment wasn't a home. It was a pit stop. And where did that leave her?

"It's not that I want to be away from you. You knew about my job right from the beginning. But we'll figure it out. I know we can make this work." He grabbed both ends of her scarf and twirled her around until she was facing him.

Despite her worries, she had to laugh at his playfulness. At his optimism. Perhaps it was too soon for her to stress about the future. He was here now. She wanted to enjoy every minute. She leaned forward to kiss him.

He pulled her close and kissed her properly. Then he said, "I'll tell you one thing all this time apart is good for. It's making me realize how much I care about you."

She waited, hoping to hear from him the words that she was feeling in her own heart.

"I've never felt like this about any other woman. I think I'm falling in love with you."

He *thought* he was falling in love? Didn't he know?

She did. She'd fallen completely for this man. So completely that she'd estranged herself from her family in order to be with him.

She didn't regret the choice she'd made, but she couldn't help worrying. Just how committed was Patrick to her?

PATRICK WOKE UP THE NEXT morning alone in his own bed. He'd hated giving up a night with Nadine, but Stephen was arriving early and he hadn't wanted to be in a position where he was rushing her out of his apartment. At some point the three of them would spend time together. But he thought it was important that he get to know Stephen one-on-one first.

Fortunately Nadine had understood. She was very sweet that way.

He leaned over to get a look at the alarm clock. Twenty minutes to nine. Stephen should be here shortly—he'd told him to grab a cab from the airport and he would cover the fare.

Patrick showered quickly and dressed in jeans and the sweater Nadine had bought him for Christmas. They'd had such a wonderful day together. Or at least he had. He hoped she had, too, but it hadn't escaped his notice that when he'd told her he thought he was falling in love, her only answer was a kiss.

The kiss had been great, but he wouldn't have minded hearing some words about love, too.

As he strapped on his watch, he noticed the time. Jeez, his son would be here any second. Maybe he'd go out to the street and wait for him.

Patrick was only outside ten minutes before a cab pulled up with a redheaded young man in the back. As Stephen stepped out to the sidewalk, Patrick leaned in to cover the tab. The driver pulled away and left them looking at one another.

His son traveled light. All he had was a backpack that didn't look very full.

"How was Christmas at your aunt's house?"

"It was okay."

"I remember my first Christmas after my mother passed away. She was my only family. It was one damn sad day."

"Yeah."

Patrick placed his arm over Stephen's shoulders. It was only then that he realized they were the exact same height. "Want to grab some breakfast? There's a good place up the street, if you like omelets."

"Sure."

Patrick dropped his arm, then headed west, toward the restaurant. Stephen stepped along beside him.

"So…I take it you finally caught up with your friend Zach?"

"Yeah. I don't think he was seriously after your money. You just caught him by surprise when you phoned."

"And he still had your mother's letter?"

Stephen snorted. "He'd forgotten all about it, if you can believe that. He had to check through all the pockets on his ski jacket before he found it."

"Thank God he hadn't sent it out for dry cleaning."

"I don't think Zach has ever cleaned that jacket. Not going by the way it smells."

Patrick laughed. "So how is your aunt Diane doing? She was just a kid when I was dating your mom. I remember they both had very different interests back then. Your mom loved sports and Diane was into ballet and piano lessons—that sort of stuff."

"She hasn't changed. She teaches music now. And she's nice enough. I just don't know her very well. We used to visit once a year, max. It was weird to spend Christmas with her."

"Everything feels weird when you've lost the person who was most important to you."

Stephen glanced at him curiously. "How old were you when your mother died?"

"Twenty-six. And it was still hard. I had a great mom."

He nodded. "Me, too." His voice broke a little on the last word. Patrick reached out for his shoulder again.

"Hey, it's sad, Stephen. It's okay to cry."

His son's lips trembled. Then he took a deep breath. "In her letter Mom said she was sorry she hadn't told me about you earlier. She said you didn't know about me."

Patrick swallowed, suddenly close to tears himself. "If I had, things would have been different."

"Yeah. Maybe."

"Definitely." His anger toward June resurfaced, and he tamped it down. "We can't change the past. But I'm here now. I want you to know that."

"I'm fine on my own."

"You may not need me, but I'd like to be a part of your life anyway. Even if it's a very small part."

Stephen hesitated before saying, "That would be okay."

Okay was good. For now, Patrick would be very happy with that.

THE NEXT MORNING, PATRICK and Stephen shared a cab to the airport. Stephen was flying back to Calgary, where he would then take a bus to Kicking Horse Resort, and Patrick was off to the next stop on his book tour—Phoenix, Arizona.

It was a good morning to be leaving New York for Arizona. The temperature had dropped ten degrees overnight and they were predicting more snow by nightfall. He and his son would be long gone by then, but Patrick couldn't help but think of the woman he was leaving behind.

He'd spoken to Nadine on the phone last night for over an hour. She'd opted out of having dinner with him and Stephen.

"This is the first time he gets to spend an entire day with his dad. I think he deserves your undivided attention."

She was right, and he had loved getting to know his son better. But he missed Nadine already and he hadn't even left.

At the airport, he walked with Stephen to the custom's line up.

"You okay? Got your passport? Enough money?"

"I'm good. Thanks again for the check. I didn't come here for money, though."

"I know." He hesitated, then gave Stephen a good, solid hug. He told himself it would be okay if it was all one-sided. The important thing was to let the boy know he really wasn't alone anymore.

But to his joy, Stephen returned the hug and even punched him on the shoulder for good measure. "Let me know when you're coming to Kicking Horse. I'll book off some time and show you around the mountain."

"I'd love that." One good thing about this next book of his. It would take him back to the mountains where his son was spending the winter.

As Stephen was turning to leave, Patrick remembered something he'd wanted to ask him. He put a hand on his son's shoulder.

"I have a favor to ask of you."

"Yeah?" Stephen tipped his head to one side, his expression cautious.

"The letter your mom wrote to you…is there any

chance you could let me read that one day?" Patrick hesitated, realizing that he might be asking for too much. "I'll understand if you want to keep it private, I just—"

"Sure." Stephen shrugged. "I'll mail you a copy when I get home."

CHAPTER TWENTY

NADINE WAS SUPPOSED TO BE on vacation for the week between Christmas and New Year's Day. But on Monday morning she couldn't help herself—she got out of bed and dressed for the office. Patrick had been gone for two days now and she was bored and lonely. She and her mother usually shopped the sales in the week after Christmas, but this year that wasn't going to happen.

She'd tried shopping on her own, but it was no fun. The only good thing was that she found the perfect shoes to go with Lindsay's wedding dress.

She wondered if her mother had gone shopping on her own, too. Was she missing her daughter? Nadine knew she must be.

Obviously both her parents felt very strongly that Patrick was the wrong man for her. In all honesty, she was beginning to appreciate their concerns. She hadn't realized how much traveling he did. How much time she would be alone.

It was not going to be easy to love this man. He would be gone often, meeting new people, doing exciting things. She imagined there would be a lot of important moments in the future that he would be absent for. Perhaps birthdays, anniversaries, days when she wasn't feeling well and needed some TLC.

Who would be there for her?

Not her parents—she'd cut off her ties with them. She'd given up the most important relationships in her life in order to be with a man who was hardly ever here. A man who may or may not be in love with her, who had only said he *thought* he was falling in love with her.

As she walked across the park toward the office, Nadine wondered if she'd made a mistake. Her life, once so normal and comfortable, felt completely out of control.

And yet, just the thought of living without Patrick, never seeing him again, never making love, was enough to make her break out in a sweat. She didn't need to wonder one way or the other. She knew she was in love with him with the same certainty that told her she would never in her life meet anyone else she could feel so passionately about.

When she arrived at the office, Nadine expected to be the only one there, but Tamara was making coffee.

"This machine is such a pain. We should get one of those instant models where you just press a button and—presto—there's your coffee."

"It's actually not that complicated." Nadine hung up her coat, then went to demonstrate. But instead of watching, and perhaps learning how to do it herself, Tamara simply returned to her desk.

"Have you heard from Lindsay or Nathan? Are they going to be in the office today?" Nadine wasn't sure how she was going to fill her time. Maybe she'd just use the day to reorganize her file cabinet.

"They're in the conference room. Going over last-minute details for the wedding." She rolled her eyes as if nothing could be more mundane.

Holding back a frown, Nadine went to the boardroom door and knocked. "Do you guys need any help?"

The door flew open. Lindsay looked panicked. "Nadine. Thank goodness. I'm going crazy, and Nathan isn't helping at all." She pointed to her fiancé who was comfortably seated, feet propped on an adjacent chair, eating a bagel.

"What's to stress about? We purposefully kept things simple. We've got the license and we've booked the officiant. The restaurant is reserved and you have your dress and I have my suit."

"We haven't given the restaurant our final guest count. Weren't we supposed to do that before Christmas?"

"I don't think there have been any changes. We've got Kate, Jay, Eric and Alice."

Lindsay ticked off the names in her notebook. "Alice doesn't count. She doesn't need a chair."

"Then there's family—my sister and nephew and your sister. Is Meg bringing a date?"

"No. What about Mary-Beth?"

"According to her, all she has time for is teaching and looking after Justin."

"Right. No date. So back to our guest list, I guess that leaves Nadine and Patrick."

"Just me," Nadine corrected.

"You couldn't talk him into flying back to the city?" Lindsay asked.

"I tried. But no luck. He won't be back in the city until mid-January."

"But—we're getting married New Year's Eve. He can't come home for New Year's?"

"Apparently not." She smiled glumly.

"That sucks." Lindsay wrinkled her nose sympathetically, then crossed his name off her list.

"Yeah, it's too bad." Tamara was standing by the open door, apparently having overheard the entire conversation. "But if you've got an extra table setting, I'm free that night."

THE NEXT DAY AT WORK WAS better. Two clients called for appointments and since Lindsay and Nathan were distracted by their upcoming wedding, Nadine was able to convince them to give her both jobs.

Suddenly she had more work than time, and Nadine was glad. She was tired of sitting at home and missing Patrick. If she couldn't be with the man she loved, at least she could spend her time productively, helping others.

Four days before the wedding, she was sitting at home in front of the computer, writing up a final report, when Patrick called.

As always, her stomach tightened with excitement when she heard his voice. She curled up on the sofa, wanting to be comfortable since their calls usually lasted an hour or longer.

"How are you doing?" he asked.

"Better. I have two new cases. The work is keeping me occupied."

"And out of trouble, I hope…"

She laughed. "How about you?"

He sighed heavily. "You don't know how sick I'm getting of giving this same presentation over and over, meeting new people every day, trying to remember names and matching them to the right faces."

She almost felt sorry for him, until she remembered

that this was his choice. No one forced him to do these tours. "Selling lots of books?"

"Yeah," he said, "but that doesn't make up for the fact that you're not here."

"I know." She was glad to be busy with work, but even that couldn't fill the void of Patrick's absence.

"I had an idea," Patrick said. "I hope you don't think it's too crazy…"

She sat upright, suddenly hopeful. Maybe he'd changed his mind about traveling back for the wedding?

"I'm going to be in Seattle tomorrow. Maybe you could fly out to meet me? I know you have to be back for the wedding, but we could have our own New Year's celebration one night early. What do you think?"

She was so disappointed, she could hardly speak. Finally she mustered an incredulous question. "You want me to fly across the country for one night?"

"It's not that crazy. You suggested I do the same thing to go to the wedding."

"That's not the same thing."

"I don't see the distinction. I thought it was a great idea."

Nadine didn't get angry easily. But this was just too much. "Sure, you think it's a great idea. Because you're not inconvenienced in the slightest, are you?"

"Nadine—"

"You want me to take a day off work, even though I'm extremely busy, and fly across the country just to spend one night with you. But you aren't willing to take the same trip to spend New Year's Eve, *and* attend my good friends' wedding, with me."

"It's not that I'm not willing. I'm locked in to a schedule here. If I had any choice—"

"You're trying to sell books, Patrick. Not negotiating peace in the Middle East. I think I'm beginning to understand why June didn't tell you that she was pregnant."

"What?"

That had been a low blow. But she wasn't going to apologize. She'd had it with this guy who *thought* he was falling in love with her and then expected her to make her life crazy in order to spend the occasional day in his company.

"I don't have time to talk anymore," she said. "I have an early appointment with a client tomorrow and I need to finish my report. Good night, Patrick."

She hung up the phone with a shaking hand and a sick, sad feeling. How could he have asked that of her? Did he really not get what she had given up for him?

Her phone rang again, almost right away. It was him, and she didn't answer.

THE NEXT DAY PATRICK RECEIVED an e-mail from his son. He was sprawled on the bed in yet another impersonal hotel room, with his laptop in front of him. Playing on the TV was a movie he'd already seen—he thought it was on the overnight in Phoenix.

He'd been checking his e-mail with the hope that he would have something from Nadine. He'd tried calling her about ten times since she'd hung up on him, but hadn't been able to reach her. He'd even tried her office, but Tamara had told him that Nadine was too busy to talk to him.

The message from Stephen had an attachment, but it wasn't until he'd opened it and saw the salutation at the top that he recognized its importance.

This was June's letter.

He reached for the glass of Scotch by his bed, polished off the contents, then started to read:

Dear Stephen,

Writing this letter to you is the hardest thing I've ever done because when you read it, I'll be gone. I'm not worried about myself, it's knowing that you will be alone that makes me sad.

I realize you have your aunt Diane and uncle Reggie, but that's not the same thing as a parent, is it? And that's why I've decided, after all these years, to tell you about your father.

Patrick O'Neil and I dated during our last year of high school. We both loved skiing and we would go out to the mountains at every opportunity. I think we were more good friends than anything else, which is why when I became pregnant, I didn't even consider that we might get married, or even that we could share you.

Your father was a good guy, lots of fun and very athletic, but he was also quite selfish. Basically he did what he wanted to do, when he wanted to do it. He dreamed of traveling—not just a summer in Europe or Thailand—he wanted to spend his life that way. He had a hunger for new places and experiences and was one of the most physically adventurous people I have ever known.

I couldn't imagine Patrick being a responsible father. And I wanted to spare you—and in all honesty, me, too—the pain of years of disappointment.

That was why I told you your father was gone. You assumed I meant dead, and I never corrected you.

Your father and I haven't been in touch for over a decade, but I've followed his career. He has done exactly what he said he would do. He's traveled to every continent in the world and written travel books for people who share his love of exploration.

I've watched his career from afar all these years, waiting to see some sign that he might be changing, growing tired of a vagabond life. But he remained the same old Patrick and I felt that I had made the right decision in keeping you apart.

Now that I'm sick, I second-guess myself. I think maybe a part-time, unreliable father is better than no father at all?

At any rate, I can't leave you without giving you a choice. If you're reading this now, it's because your father cared enough to track you down. You see, I've sent him a letter, too, which I asked a friend of mine from work to mail after I was gone. I imagine he'll be shocked to find out he has a son. And I expect he'll have some anger toward me for keeping this secret.

Maybe you'll be angry at me, too.

But I hope you'll forgive me eventually. And I hope you will take a chance on your father. I would love to know that he is looking out for you. That's what I choose to believe will happen.

Stephen, my body will fail me soon, but the

closer I come to my final day, the more certain I am
that one thing will never die, and that is my love for
you. Be strong, son, and most important, be happy.

CHAPTER TWENTY-ONE

PATRICK'S GUT BURNED AS HE read June's letter a second time, then a third. Her words hadn't been meant for him, but they still hurt.

How dared she condemn him and his lifestyle? Surely it wasn't selfish to pursue your dreams and live your life to the fullest. He hadn't known about the baby—it wasn't fair to judge his life the way she had. So what if he'd done exactly what he wanted? He'd had no obligations, nothing tying him down.

Yeah, really? What about Mom?

He got out of bed and started to pace. It was true he had regrets where his mother was concerned. She'd undoubtedly missed him during his long absences. And when she'd found out she was sick—she'd never asked him to come back and live with her during her final months. But perhaps she had secretly wished that he would.

He'd been twenty-five when his mother was first diagnosed with cancer. She'd assured him she would beat it, but by his twenty-sixth birthday she was gone.

Patrick went to the window, pushed aside the curtains. For a moment he'd forgotten where he was, then he recognized the Space Needle. Seattle.

He thought about Nadine, who had refused to meet

him here. He'd spent the day hoping she would change her mind, that when he checked into the hotel at night he would find her waiting for him.

But, of course, she hadn't been here. Like June, she thought he was selfish. Neither one of them understood that not all jobs fit neatly into nine-to-five slots.

His book tours were a pain, but they helped with book sales, and book sales funded his adventures. It wasn't a sin to spend your life engaged in work that made you happy.

No. But what about balance? What about considering the needs of the people you love?

Maybe as a young man it was all right to focus on your own needs. But he was thirty-six years old. There was a son in his life now. And a woman.

He'd never felt about anyone the way he felt about Nadine.

If he really loved her, then shouldn't making *her* happy be the most important thing?

THE ONLY CONVENTIONAL ASPECT of Lindsay and Nathan's wedding was the bridal dress. Nadine fingered the white silk, which felt as soft as Alice's skin. "Do you want me to lift it over your head? Or would you rather step into it?"

Nadine and Lindsay's sister, Meg, were helping the bride dress. Kate was watching from the sofa where she was breast-feeding Alice.

They were in Lindsay and Nathan's apartment— Nathan having gone to Jay and Kate's to get ready.

Lindsay stood frozen to the floor, dressed in her fine French bra and panties and the delectable Vera Wang silver-white pumps Nadine had found for her.

"I can't do this," she said.

"Yes, you can," Meg insisted.

"I don't have anything borrowed, and nothing blue. I *knew* I was going to forget something."

"I didn't think you cared about those silly old customs," Meg said in her best analytical lawyer tone.

Meg was a finer-featured, thinner, more delicate version of her older sister. It was from her successful, Midtown practice that many of their clients were referred.

"Except for the dress. And borrowed and blue are part of the dress. Nadine, isn't that right? I don't want to jinx this marriage before it even starts."

"I have it covered," Nadine said calmly. Like Meg, she hadn't thought Lindsay would worry about the finer details, but just in case she'd brought along her mother's blue lace handkerchief.

She'd found it in the cedar box that her mother had packed for her when she'd moved into her own apartment. The hankie was meant for her to wear at her own wedding, but Nadine had serious doubts that that day would ever come.

She couldn't imagine loving anyone but Patrick.

And she couldn't see a future with him, either. It wasn't healthy for her to be the one who always gave, who always compromised. Much as she needed Patrick, she would not be part of such an unbalanced relationship.

After that awful fight, when she'd said those awful things, he'd tried to call her a bunch of times the next day. But less than twenty-four hours later, he'd stopped calling completely.

She wondered if he'd met someone else. It was certainly possible. It would *always* be possible given the life he led.

"That's perfect, Nadine." Lindsay held the handkerchief gently. "But where do I put it?"

"Let's get the dress on first," Meg said patiently. "You'd better step in so you don't mess up your hair."

"Thanks, Meg." Lindsay moved as directed, then held up her arms. "Now do the zip. And all those little buttons…"

Lindsay's dress was strapless and hugged her body like a second skin.

"We'll tuck the hankie in your glove," Nadine said. "There. You look beautiful."

Beyond beautiful, really. With her pale blond hair, flawless skin and light blue eyes, Lindsay could look ethereal when she wasn't busy kicking someone's butt or working a case.

Lindsay checked out her reflection. "Not bad."

"And perfect timing." Meg checked her watch. "The limo should be waiting downstairs. Kate, do you need a few more minutes?"

"No, thanks. Alice is a fast eater…like her father." Kate bundled the baby in a snowsuit, then buckled her into a car seat. "Nadine, do you mind grabbing the diaper bag for me? I'm afraid my days of traveling light are over."

"No problem." Nadine took Lindsay's overnight bag, as well, since she and Nathan were staying in a ritzy downtown hotel for their wedding night.

The honeymoon in New Zealand wasn't going to happen until Kate returned from mat leave.

It was almost eight when they arrived at the Garden

Restaurant, which was on the top floor of a forty-story building and had a fabulous city view.

The ceremony was supposed to be simple. Just an exchange of vows and rings, with no music or bridesmaids or processions of any kind. "I'd burst out laughing if I had to walk down an aisle," Lindsay had said, and Nathan had agreed it wasn't her style.

"As long as we are legally husband and wife by the end of the evening, I'll be a very happy man."

And it looked as if he was going to get his wish, Nadine thought, as she entered the reserved room ahead of the others. A long, rectangular table was set up in one corner for the meal. The officiant was standing by the window, conversing with Nathan.

The other guests were milling around the bar. Nadine smiled at Jay and Eric. "Kate and Alice are right behind me," she assured them. "Kate wanted to stop in the washroom to change the baby's diaper."

"And Lindsay?" Nathan asked.

"Meg's putting the finishing touches on her makeup. She'll be right in."

Noticing that the others had glasses of champagne in hand, Nadine headed for the bar. She wanted to be ready for the toast when the short ceremony was over.

She walked up to a woman who had dark, curly hair and a warm smile. "You must be Nathan's sister."

"Yes, I'm Mary-Beth. And you must be Nadine. It's so nice to meet you. This is my son, Justin." She placed her hand on the head of a towheaded toddler. "He usually goes to bed around now, so this should be interesting."

Nadine crouched to say hello to the little guy. His

eyes were bright and she guessed adrenaline was going to keep him going for a while, yet.

As she rose, she became aware of someone else in the room. He was standing in shadow, in the far corner, and…

"Oh my God." It couldn't be him, could it?

But then he smiled and she had no doubt.

It was Patrick. Somehow he had managed to make it to the wedding.

THE MOMENT NADINE RECOGNIZED him Patrick knew all the organizing and phone calls and pleading and re-scheduling had been worth it.

"I hope you don't mind that I surprised you. I wasn't sure, at first, if I was going to be able to make it. My connection was really tight. And then my flight into New York was delayed by almost an hour. I was afraid all my planning would be for nothing."

"I can't believe you're really here." She touched the sleeve of his jacket tentatively.

She was happy to see him, he could tell by the way her face glowed. Though, as far as he was concerned, Nadine always had a special light around her.

He drew her close and kissed her. "It's so wonderful to be here."

"What made you decide to come?"

"I realized this was an important occasion. And that I should be here to share it with you. I want to share all your important occasions, Nadine. And the not-so-important ones, too."

"Does this mean you're no longer 'falling'…but that you've actually fallen?"

It took him a minute to understand what she was

asking. Then he realized, ruefully, that he should have been more specific with his language the first time. "I've been in love with you practically from the moment we met."

She grasped his lapels in her hands and pulled him in tightly. "I love you, too, Patrick. I love you like crazy." Then the light in her eyes dimmed a bit. "How long until you have to leave?"

"I've only got twenty-four hours," he confessed. "And then only a month before I need to go to Canada. But I've decided that this is going to be my last book. I might even have tried to get out of this contract, but I'm hoping I'll get to spend time with Stephen when I'm doing my research."

"What do you mean, your last book?"

"I mean, I don't want to live away from you for most of the year. I'm going to find a regular job. Maybe something in the magazine business. I have lots of contacts in the publishing world. I should be able to find something."

"Really? That would be so wonderful…but will you be happy? Won't you miss the travel and the adventure?"

"Traveling is a young man's sport. And I'm thinking making a new life with you might be enough of an adventure. What do you think, sweetheart? Are you up for the challenge of having me around every morning, and every night, and full-time on the weekends?"

"Patrick, that sounds very much like you're asking me…"

"If you'll marry me. Yes, that's exactly what I want. With children in the package, too, if that's okay."

"Oh, babies would be wonderful."

"Hopefully by then I'll have won over your parents."

"I hope so, too. But either way, you've already won over me."

This had to be the happiest moment of his life so far. He had great hopes that there would be more of them. But someone else had center stage now.

He leaned over to whisper into Nadine's ear. "A lady in a long white dress just came into the room. I think we'd better give her our attention for a little bit."

PATRICK KNEW HIS OWN JOY colored his perception of the ceremony, but it seemed like the most perfect wedding he'd ever attended. It didn't hurt that it was over quickly. Once the vows and rings had been exchanged, Nathan proposed a toast to his bride, then Lindsay returned the favor.

"Now it's time for good food, good drink and good times," she concluded, laughing as she linked arms with Nathan and invited everyone to take their place around the table.

As people shuffled around, checking place cards, and finding the appropriate spot, a woman came up beside him.

"Are you Patrick O'Neil?"

"Yes. Why?"

She helped her son into a chair with a booster seat, then brushed her hair back from her eyes. "It sure is a small world. I used to teach at Columbia University. A very good friend of mine, someone you knew, taught there, as well, but she passed away recently."

The color leached out of Patrick's face. "You knew June Stone?"

"Yes. I'm the one who mailed her letters to you."

Patrick tightened his grip on Nadine's hand, then realized he must be hurting her. But she said nothing. She, too, was astonished by Mary-Beth's pronouncement.

"You mailed the letters? But what a coincidence that we should meet this way."

"It isn't a coincidence at all," Nadine realized. "Mary-Beth is Nathan's sister. And Nathan is who June told you to look for if you wanted to find Stephen."

"I take it you *did* track down your son?"

"It wasn't easy." Patrick gave Nadine a private smile. "But yes, with Nadine's help."

"I'm sorry. I gather Stephen took off shortly after June's funeral. Her death will be hard on him—they were very close. I'm glad you're willing to be a part of his life now."

"Frankly, I wish I'd had the opportunity sooner." June had called him selfish, and he wasn't denying that was the case. But he liked to think he would have responded to unplanned parenthood with more maturity than she had given him credit for.

Mary-Beth sighed. "It isn't easy being an unmarried mother. Don't be too upset with June."

He could only imagine the sacrifices that she must have made. "Fair enough."

He pulled out a seat for Nadine, then sat in the chair next to her. Mary-Beth settled beside him.

"June almost changed her mind about those letters. I was with her on her last day. She told me she was losing her nerve. I managed to convince her that it was the right thing."

"I'm glad you did." Patrick watched Nadine tuck her hair behind her ears, as she leaned forward to read the menu. Not only had June's letters connected him with his son, but it had led him to his future wife, as well.

Maybe things had worked out exactly as they were supposed to, after all.

* * * * *

Harlequin offers a romance for every mood!
See below for a sneak peek
from our paranormal romance line,
Silhouette® Nocturne™.
Enjoy a preview of REUNION by USA TODAY
bestselling author Lindsay McKenna.

Aella closed her eyes and sensed a distinct shift, like movement from the world around her to the unseen world.

She opened her eyes. And had a slight shock at the man standing ten feet away. He wasn't just any man. Her heart leaped and pounded. He reminded her of a fierce warrior from an ancient civilization. Incan? She wasn't sure but she felt his deep power and masculinity.

I'm Aella. Are you the guardian of this sacred site? she asked, hoping her telepathy was strong.

Fox's entire body soared with joy. Fox struggled to put his personal pleasure aside.

Greetings, Aella. I'm the assistant guardian to this sacred area. You may call me Fox. How can I be of service to you, Aella? he asked.

I'm searching for a green sphere. A legend says that the Emperor Pachacuti had seven emerald spheres created for the Emerald Key necklace. He had seven of his priestesses and priests travel the world to hide these spheres from evil forces. It is said that when all seven spheres are found, restrung and worn, that Light will return to the Earth. The fourth sphere is here, at your sacred site. Are you aware of it? Aella held her breath.

She loved looking at him, especially his sensual mouth. The desire to kiss him came out of nowhere.

Fox was stunned by the request. *I know of the Emerald Key necklace because I served the emperor at the time it was created. However, I did not realize that one of the spheres is here.*

Aella felt sad. Why? Every time she looked at Fox, her heart felt as if it would tear out of her chest. *May I stay in touch with you as I work with this site?* she asked.

Of course. Fox wanted nothing more than to be here with her. To absorb her ephemeral beauty and hear her speak once more.

Aella's spirit lifted. What *was* this strange connection between them? Her curiosity was strong, but she had more pressing matters. In the next few days, Aella knew her life would change forever. How, she had no idea....

Look for REUNION
by USA TODAY bestselling author
Lindsay McKenna,
available April 2010, only from
Silhouette® Nocturne™.

HARLEQUIN® *Romance*®

ROMANCE, RIVALRY
AND A FAMILY REUNITED

THE BRIDES
of
BELLA ROSA

William Valentine and his beloved wife, Lucia, live
a beautiful life together, but when his former love Rosa
and the secret family they had together resurface,
an instant rivalry is formed. Can these families
get through the past and come together as one?

Step into the world of Bella Rosa
beginning this April with

Beauty and the Reclusive Prince
by

RAYE MORGAN

Eight volumes to collect and treasure!

www.eHarlequin.com

HR17650

LARGER-PRINT BOOKS!
GET 2 FREE LARGER-PRINT NOVELS PLUS
2 FREE GIFTS!

HARLEQUIN®

Super Romance®

Exciting, emotional, unexpected!

YES! Please send me 2 FREE LARGER-PRINT Harlequin® Superromance® novels and my 2 FREE gifts (gifts are worth about $10). After receiving them, if I don't wish to receive any more books, I can return the shipping statement marked "cancel." If I don't cancel, I will receive 6 brand-new novels every month and be billed just $5.44 per book in the U.S. or $5.99 per book in Canada. That's a saving of over 15% off the cover price! It's quite a bargain! Shipping and handling is just 50¢ per book in the U.S. and 75¢ per book in Canada.* I understand that accepting the 2 free books and gifts places me under no obligation to buy anything. I can always return a shipment and cancel at any time. Even if I never buy another book from Harlequin, the two free books and gifts are mine to keep forever.

139 HDN E4JY   339 HDN E4KC

Name _____ (PLEASE PRINT) _____

Address _____ Apt. # _____

City _____ State/Prov. _____ Zip/Postal Code _____

Signature (if under 18, a parent or guardian must sign) _____

Mail to the **Harlequin Reader Service:**
IN U.S.A.: P.O. Box 1867, Buffalo, NY 14240-1867
IN CANADA: P.O. Box 609, Fort Erie, Ontario L2A 5X3

Not valid for current subscribers to Harlequin Superromance Larger-Print books.

Are you a current subscriber to Harlequin Superromance books and want to receive the larger-print edition?
Call 1-800-873-8635 today!

* Terms and prices subject to change without notice. Prices do not include applicable taxes. N.Y. residents add applicable sales tax. Canadian residents will be charged applicable provincial taxes and GST. Offer not valid in Quebec. This offer is limited to one order per household. All orders subject to approval. Credit or debit balances in a customer's account(s) may be offset by any other outstanding balance owed by or to the customer. Please allow 4 to 6 weeks for delivery. Offer available while quantities last.

Your Privacy: Harlequin Books is committed to protecting your privacy. Our Privacy Policy is available online at www.eHarlequin.com or upon request from the Reader Service. From time to time we make our lists of customers available to reputable third parties who may have a product or service of interest to you. If you would prefer we not share your name and address, please check here. ☐

Help us get it right—We strive for accurate, respectful and relevant communications. To clarify or modify your communication preferences, visit us at www.ReaderService.com/consumerschoice.

HSRLP10

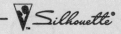
Silhouette®

SPECIAL EDITION

**INTRODUCING A BRAND-NEW MINISERIES
FROM *USA TODAY* BESTSELLING AUTHOR**

KASEY MICHAELS

SECOND-CHANCE
BRIDAL

At twenty-eight, widowed single mother
Elizabeth Carstairs thinks she's left love behind
forever....until she meets Will Hollingsbrook.
Her sons' new baseball coach is the handsomest
man she's ever seen—and the more time they
spend together, the more undeniable the
connection between them. But can Elizabeth
leave the past behind and open her heart to
a second chance at love?

FIND OUT IN

SUDDENLY A BRIDE

*Available in April
wherever books are sold.*

Visit Silhouette Books at www.eHarlequin.com

SSE65517

COMING NEXT MONTH

Available April 13, 2010